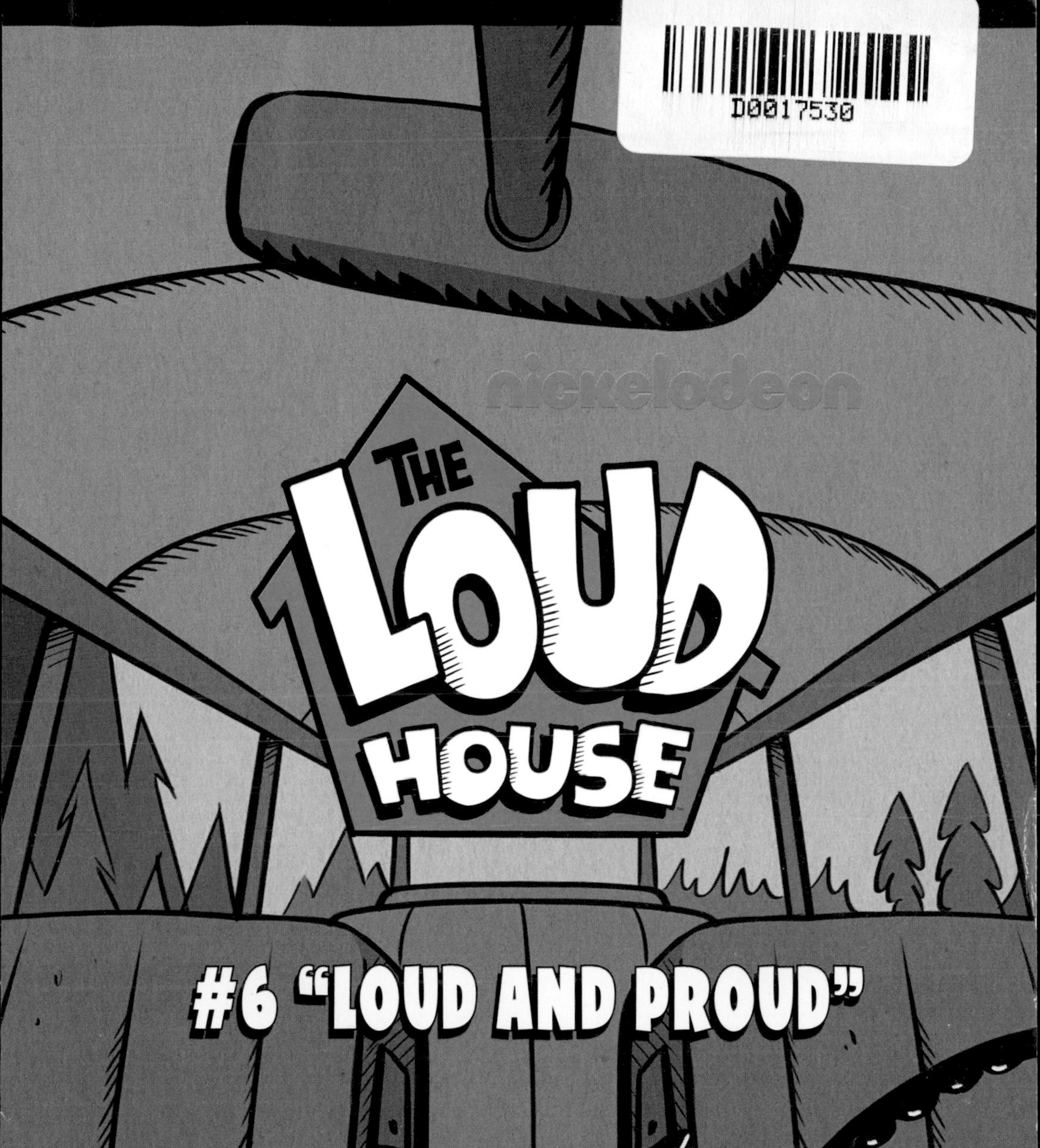

nickelodeon

THE LOUD HOUSE

#6 "LOUD AND PROUD"

PAPERCUTZ
New York

nickelodeon GRAPHIC NOVELS AVAILABLE FROM PAPERCUTZ

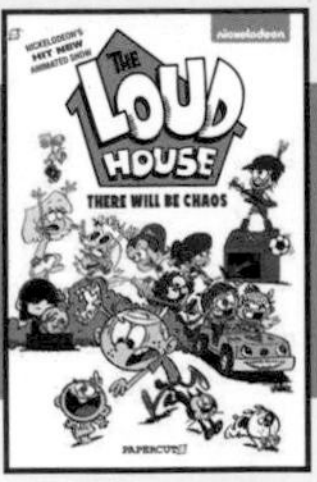
THE LOUD HOUSE
THERE WILL BE CHAOS

THE LOUD HOUSE
#1
"There Will Be Chaos"

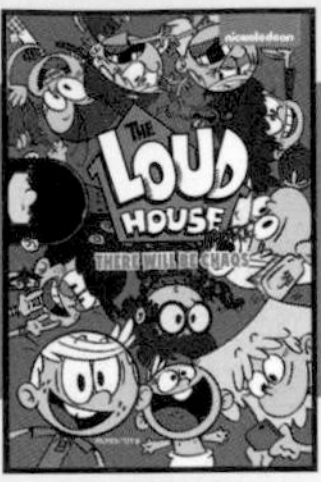
THE LOUD HOUSE

THE LOUD HOUSE
#2
"There Will Be More Chaos"

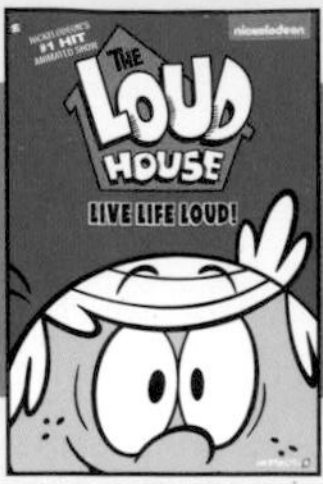
THE LOUD HOUSE
LIVE LIFE LOUD!

THE LOUD HOUSE
#3
"Live Life Loud!"

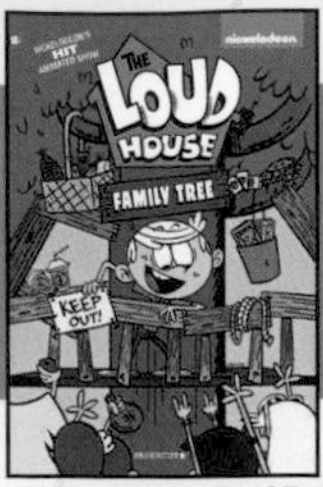
THE LOUD HOUSE
FAMILY TREE
KEEP OUT!

THE LOUD HOUSE
#4
"Family Tree"

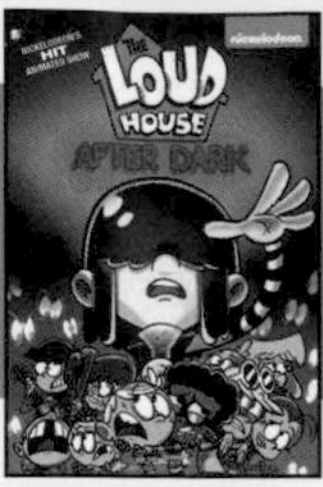
THE LOUD HOUSE
AFTER DARK

THE LOUD HOUSE
#5
"After Dark"

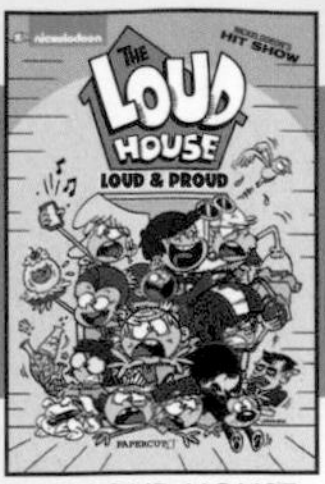
THE LOUD HOUSE
LOUD & PROUD

THE LOUD HOUSE
#6
"Loud and Proud"

COMING SOON

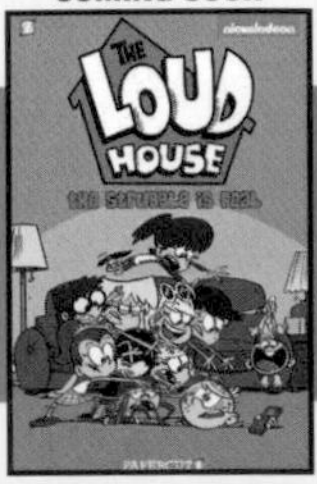
THE LOUD HOUSE

THE LOUD HOUSE
#7
"The Struggle is Real"

COMING SOON

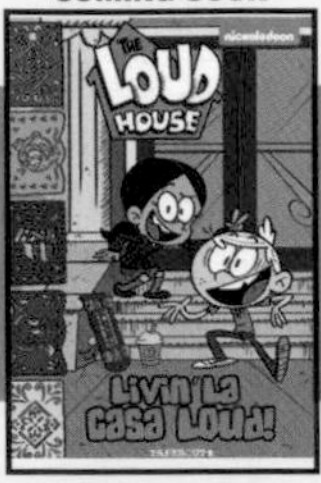
THE LOUD HOUSE
Livin' La Casa Loud!

THE LOUD HOUSE
#8
"Livin' La Casa Loud"

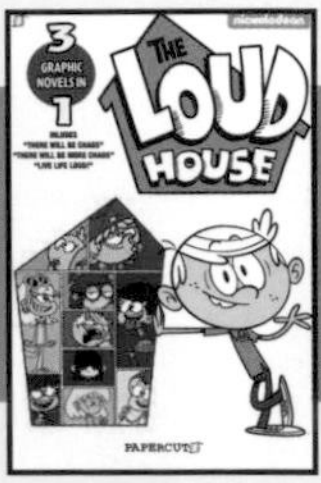
3 GRAPHIC NOVELS IN 1
THE LOUD HOUSE

THE LOUD HOUSE
3 IN 1
#1

COMING SOON

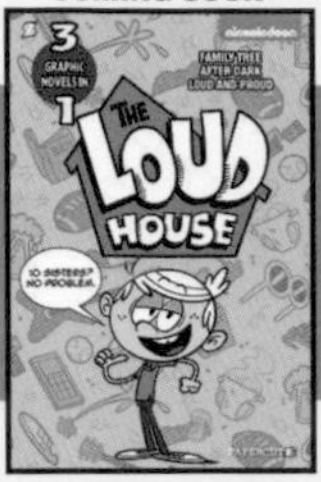
3 GRAPHIC NOVELS IN 1
THE LOUD HOUSE

THE LOUD HOUSE
3 IN 1
#2

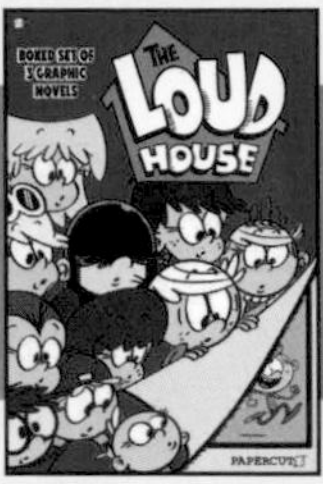
THE LOUD HOUSE

THE LOUD HOUSE
BOXED SET
$23.99

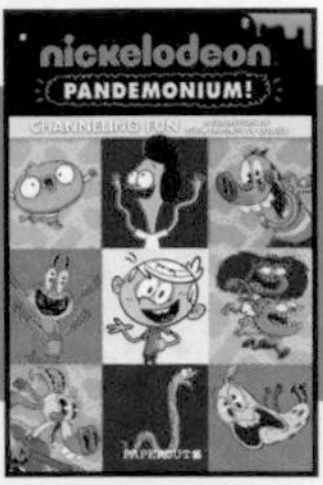
nickelodeon
PANDEMONIUM!

NICKELODEON PANDEMONIUM
#1
"Channeling Fun"

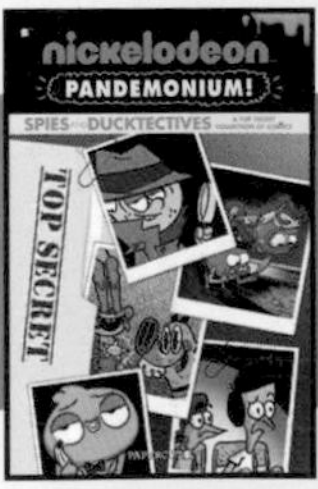
nickelodeon
PANDEMONIUM!
TOP SECRET

NICKELODEON PANDEMONIUM
#2
"Spies and Ducktectives"

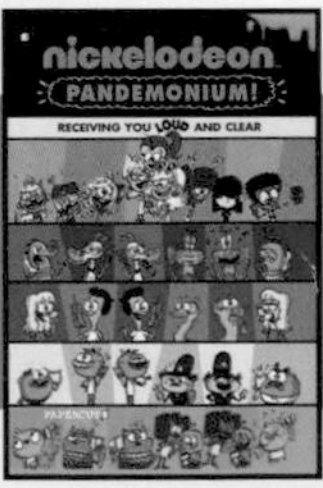
nickelodeon
PANDEMONIUM!

NICKELODEON PANDEMONIUM
#3
"Receiving You Loud and Clear"

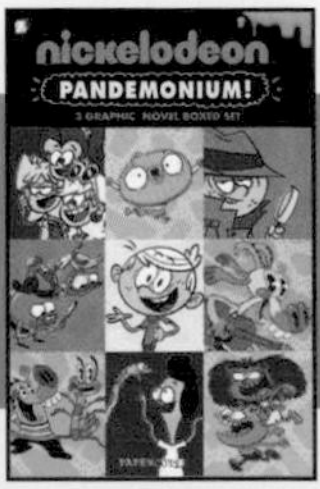
nickelodeon
PANDEMONIUM!

NICKELODEON PANDEMONIUM
BOXED SET
$24.99

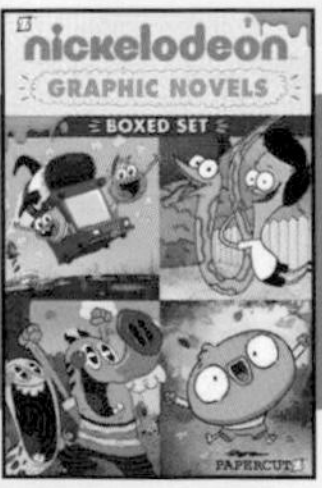
nickelodeon
GRAPHIC NOVELS
BOXED SET

NICKELODEON
BOXED SET
$31.99

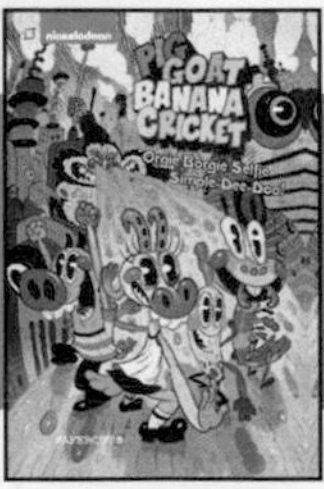
PIG GOAT BANANA CRICKET

PIG GOAT BANANA CRICKET
#1
"Orgle Borgle Selfie Simple-Dee Doo!"

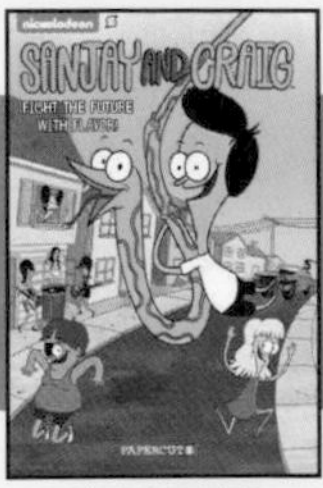
SANJAY AND CRAIG

SANJAY AND CRAIG
#1
"Fight the Future with Flavor"

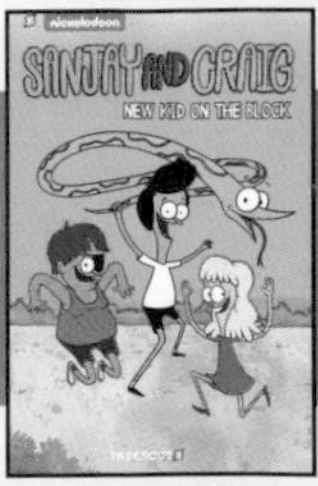
SANJAY AND CRAIG
NEW KID ON THE BLOCK

SANJAY AND CRAIG
#2
"New Kid on the Block"

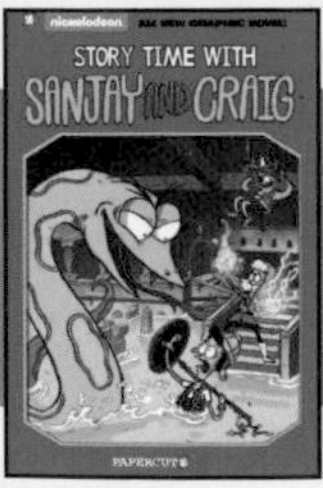
STORY TIME WITH
SANJAY AND CRAIG

SANJAY AND CRAIG
#3
"Story Time with Sanjay and Craig"

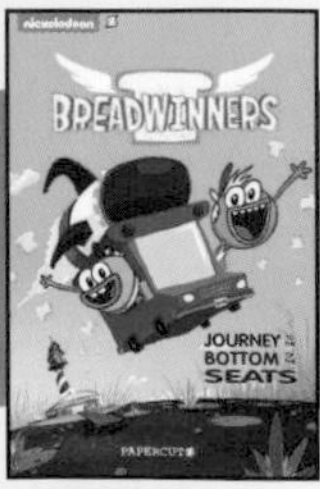
BREADWINNERS
JOURNEY TO THE BOTTOM OF THE SEATS

BREADWINNERS
#1
"Journey to the Bottom of the Seats"

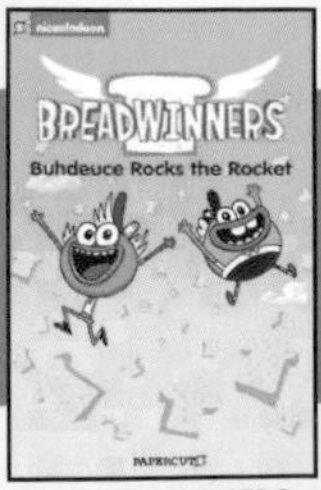
BREADWINNERS
Buhdeuce Rocks the Rocket

BREADWINNERS
#2
"Buhdeuce Rocks the Rocket"

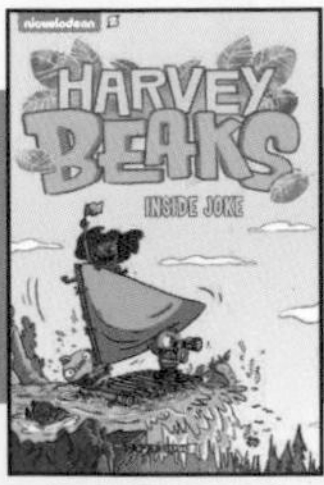
HARVEY BEAKS
INSIDE JOKE

HARVEY BEAKS
#1
"Inside Joke"

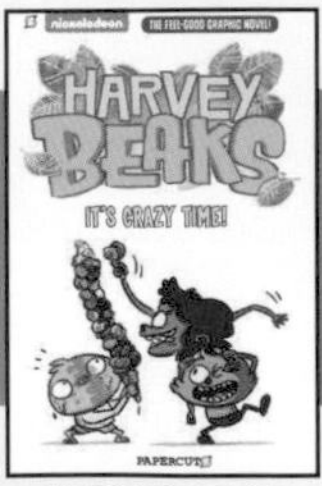
HARVEY BEAKS
IT'S CRAZY TIME!

HARVEY BEAKS
#2
"It's Crazy Time"

Nickelodeon graphic novels are available for $7.99 each in paperback, $12.99 each in hardcover. NICKELODEON PANDEMONIUM #3 is $8.99 each in paperback, $13.99 each in hardcover. BOXED SETS differ in price. Available from booksellers everywhere. You can also order online from Papercutz.com, or call 1-800-886-1223, Monday through Friday, 9-5 EST. MC, Visa, and AmEx accepted. To order by mail, please add $5.00 for postage and handling for the first book ordered, $1.00 for each additional book and make check payable to NBM Publishing.
Send to: Papercutz, 160 Broadway, Suite 700, East Wing, New York, NY 10038.

Nickelodeon graphic novels are also available digitally wherever e-books are sold.

THE LOUD HOUSE

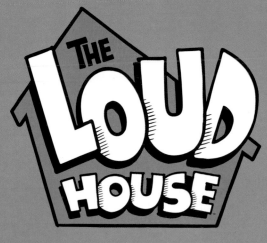

#6 "LOUD AND PROUD"

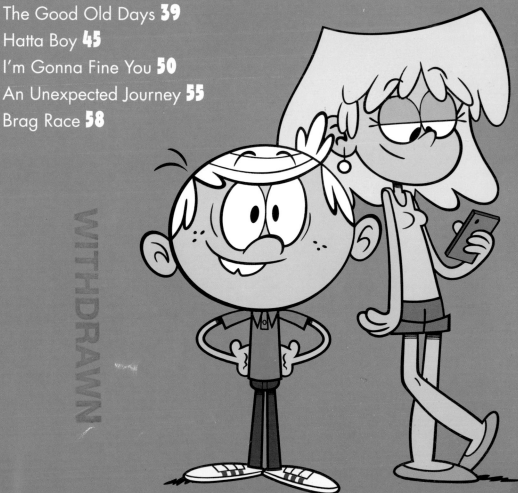

nickelodeon THE LOUD HOUSE

#6 "LOUD AND PROUD"

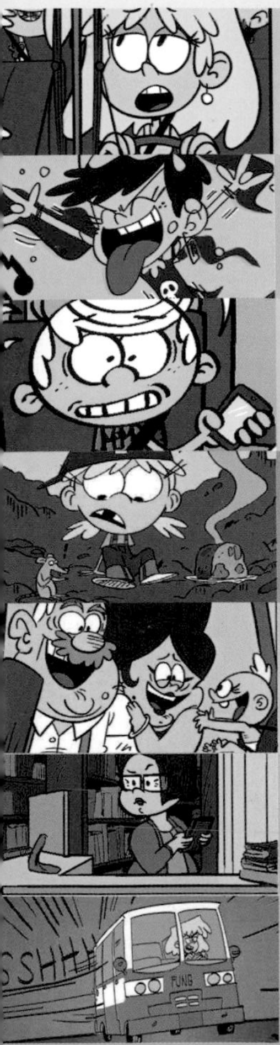

"BUCKLE UP"
Sammie Crowley—Writer
Angela Zhang—Artist, Colorist
Wilson Ramos Jr.—Letterer

"BANDS ON THE RUN"
Kevin Sullivan—Writer
Erin Hyde—Artist, Colorist
Wilson Ramos Jr.—Letterer

"HURRY UP AND WAIT"
Sammie Crowley—Writer
Colton Davis—Artist
Emily Merl—Colorist
Wilson Ramos Jr.—Letterer

"DOWN IN THE DUMPS"
Angela Entzminger—Writer
Agny Innocente—Artist
Gabrielle Dolbey—Colorist
Wilson Ramos Jr.—Letterer

"THE GOOD OLD DAYS"
Sammie Crowley—Writer
Ida Hem—Artist, Letterer
Hallie Lal—Colorist

"I'M GONNA FINE YOU"
Whitney Wetta—Writer
Suzannah Rowntree—Artist
Lauren Patterson—Colorist
Wilson Ramos Jr.—Letterer

"BRAG RACE"
Andrew Brooks—Writer
Gizelle Orbino—Artist, Colorist
Wilson Ramos Jr.—Letterer

"MALL FLOP"
Andrew Brooks—Writer
Isaiah Kim—Artist, Colorist
Wilson Ramos Jr.—Letterer

"THE PAGEANT TRAP"
Kevin Sullivan—Writer
Angela Zhang—Artist, Colorist
Wilson Ramos Jr.—Letterer

"STAGE FRIGHT"
Hannah Watanabe-Rocco—Writer
Melissa Kleynowski—Artist
Karolyn Moses—Colorist
Wilson Ramos Jr.—Letterer

"VAN GO"
Sammie Crowley—Writer
Colton Davis—Artist
Emily Merl—Colorist
Wilson Ramos Jr.—Letterer

"HATTA BOY"
Scott Tuft—Writer
Brian Smith—Artist, Colorist
Wilson Ramos Jr.—Letterer

"AN UNEXPECTED JOURNEY"
Sammie Crowley—Writer
Colton Davis—Artist
Emily Merl—Colorist
Wilson Ramos Jr.—Letterer

JORDAN KOCH—Cover Artist

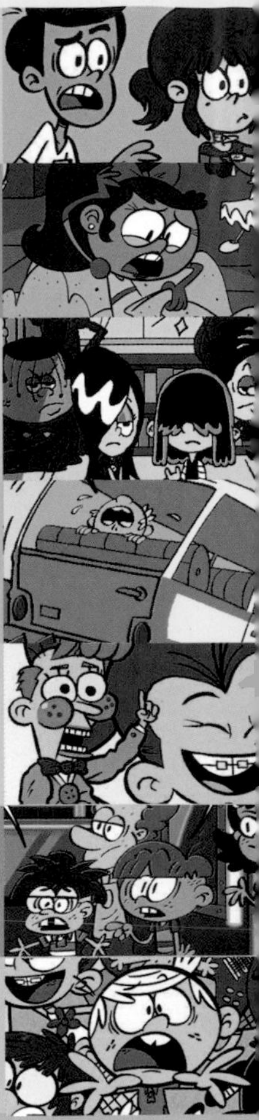

JAMES SALERNO—Sr. Art Director/Nickelodeon
JAYJAY JACKSON—Design
SEAN GANTKA, ANGELA ENTZMINGER, SAMMIE CROWLEY, DANA CLUVERIUS, MOLLIE FREILICH, AMANDA RYNDA—Special Thanks
JEFF WHITMAN—Editor
KARR ANTUNES—Editorial Intern
JOAN HILTY—Comics Editor/Nickelodeon
JIM SALICRUP
Editor-in-Chief

ISBN: 978-1-5458-0210-6 paperback edition
ISBN: 978-1-5458-0211-3 hardcover edition

www.papercutz.com

Papercutz books may be purchased for business or promotional use. For information on bulk purchases please contact Macmillan Corporate and Premium Sales Department at (800) 221-7945 x5442.

Printed in India
April 2019

Distributed by Macmillan
First Printing

MEET THE LOUD FAMILY and friends!

LINCOLN LOUD
THE MIDDLE CHILD (11)

At 11 years old, Lincoln is the middle child, with five older sisters and five younger sisters. He has learned that surviving the Loud household means staying a step ahead. He's the man with a plan, always coming up with a way to get what he wants or deal with a problem, even if things inevitably go wrong. Being the only boy comes with some perks. Lincoln gets his own room – even if it's just a converted linen closet. On the other hand, being the only boy also means he sometimes gets a little too much attention from his sisters. They mother him, tease him, and use him as the occasional lab rat or fashion show participant. Lincoln's sisters may drive him crazy, but he loves them and is always willing to help out if they need him.

LORI LOUD
THE OLDEST (17)

As the first-born child of the Loud Clan, Lori sees herself as the boss of all her siblings. She feels she's paved the way for them and deserves extra respect. Her signature traits are rolling her eyes, texting her boyfriend, Bobby, and literally saying "literally" all the time. Because she's the oldest and most experienced sibling, Lori can be a great ally, so it pays to stay on her good side, especially since she can drive.

LENI LOUD
THE FASHIONISTA (16)

Leni spends most of her time designing outfits and accessorizing. She always falls for Luan's pranks, and sometimes walks into walls when she's talking (she's not great at doing two things at once). Leni might be flighty, but she's the sweetest of the Loud siblings and truly has a heart of gold (even though she's pretty sure it's a heart of blood).

LUNA LOUD
THE ROCK STAR (15)

Luna is loud, boisterous and freewheeling, and her energy is always cranked to 11. She thinks about music so much that she even talks in song lyrics. On the off-chance she doesn't have her guitar with her, everything can and will be turned into a musical instrument. You can always count on Luna to help out, and she'll do most anything you ask, as long as you're okay with her supplying a rocking guitar accompaniment.

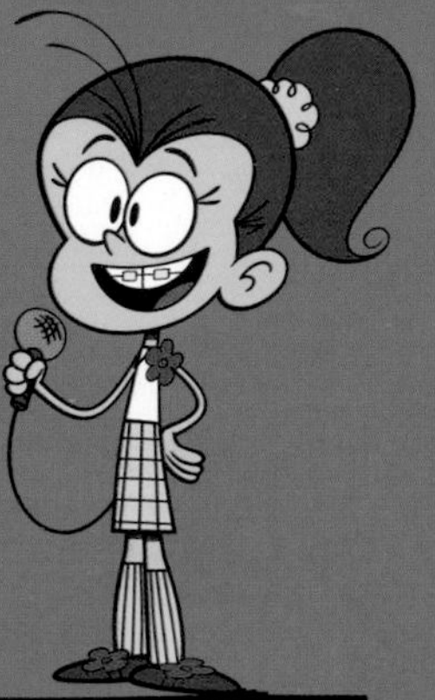

LUAN LOUD
THE JOKESTER (14)

Luan's a standup comedienne who provides a nonstop barrage of silly puns. She's big on prop comedy too – squirting flowers and whoopee cushions – so you have to be on your toes whenever she's around. She loves to pull pranks and is a really good ventriloquist – she is often found doing bits with her dummy, Mr. Coconuts. Luan never lets anything get her down; to her, laughter IS the best medicine.

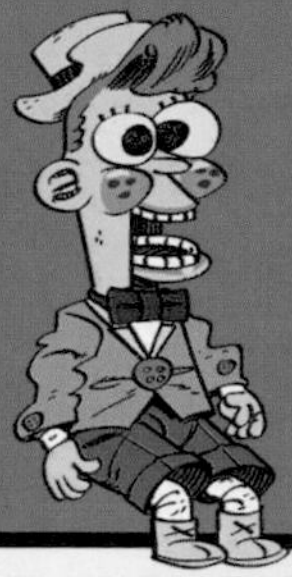

MR COCONUTS

Luan Loud's wise-cracking dummy.

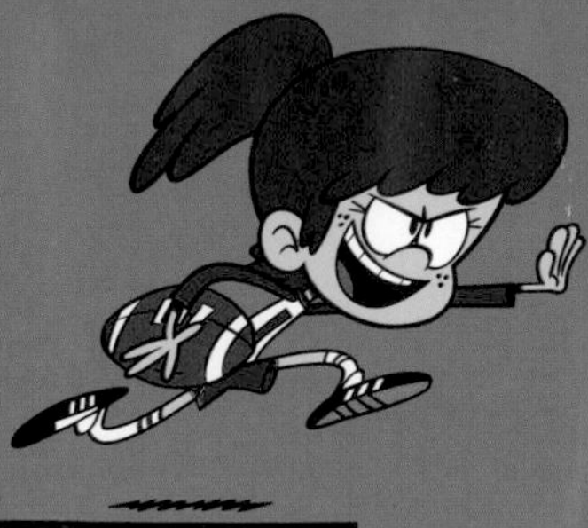

LYNN LOUD
THE ATHLETE (13)

Lynn is athletic and full of energy and is always looking for a teammate. With her, it's all sports all the time. She'll turn anything into a sport. Putting away eggs? Jump shot! Score! Cleaning up the eggs? Slap shot! Score! Lynn is very competitive, but despite her competitive nature, she always tries to just have a good time.

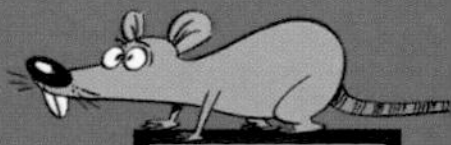

BITEY

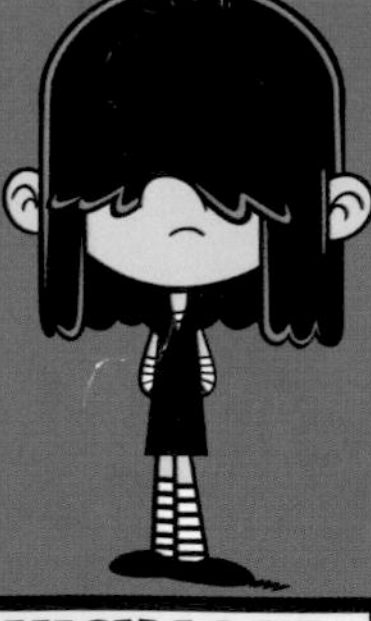

LUCY LOUD
THE EMO (8)

You can always count on Lucy to give the morbid point of view in any given situation. She is obsessed with all things spooky and dark – funerals, vampires, séances, and the like. She wears mostly black and writes moody poetry. She's usually quiet and keeps to herself. Lucy has a way of mysteriously appearing out of nowhere, and try as they might, her siblings never get used to this.

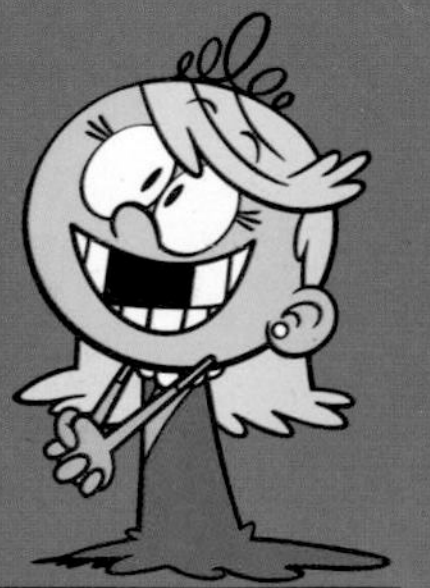

LOLA LOUD
THE BEAUTY QUEEN (6)

Lola could not be more different from her twin sister, Lana. She's a pageant powerhouse whose interests include glitter, photo shoots, and her own beautiful, beautiful face. But don't let her cute, gap-toothed smile fool you; underneath all the sugar and spice lurks a Machiavellian mastermind. Whatever Lola wants, Lola gets – or else. She's the eyes and ears of the household and never resists an opportunity to tattle on troublemakers. But if you stay on Lola's good side, you've got yourself a fierce ally – and a lifetime supply of free makeovers.

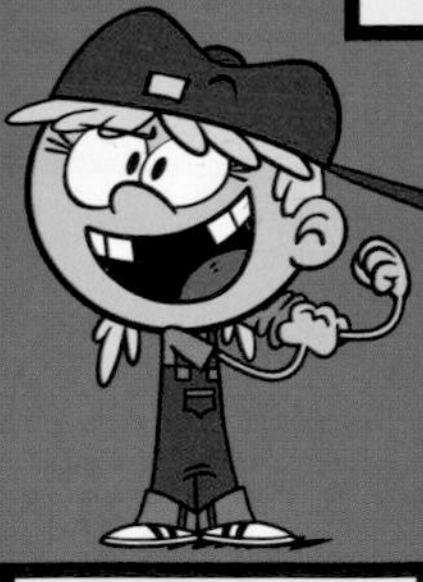

LANA LOUD
THE TOMBOY (6)

Lana is the rough-and-tumble sparkplug counterpart to her twin sister, Lola. She's all about reptiles, mud pies, and muffler repair. She's the resident Ms. Fix-it and is always ready to lend a hand – the dirtier the job, the better. Need your toilet unclogged? Snake fed? Back-zit popped? Lana's your gal. All she asks in return is a little A-B-C gum, or a handful of kibble (she often sneaks it from the dog bowl).

LISA LOUD
THE GENIUS (4)

Lisa is smarter than the rest of her siblings combined. She'll most likely be a rocket scientist, or a brain surgeon, or an evil genius who takes over the world. Lisa spends most of her time working in her lab (the family has gotten used to the explosions), and says her research leaves little time for frivolous human pursuits like "playing" or "getting haircuts." That said, she's always there to help with a homework question, or to explain why the sky is blue, or to point out the structural flaws in someone's pillow fort. Lisa says it's the least she can do for her favorite test subjects, er, siblings.

LILY LOUD
THE BABY (15 MONTHS)

Lily is a giggly, drooly, diaper-ditching free spirit, affectionately known as "the poop machine." You can't keep a nappy on this kid – she's like a teething Houdini. But even when Lily's running wild, dropping rancid diaper bombs, or drooling all over the remote, she always brings a smile to everyone's face (and a clothespin to their nose). Lily is everyone's favorite little buddy, and the whole family loves her unconditionally.

RITA LOUD

Mother to the eleven Loud kids, Mom (Rita Loud) wears many different hats. She's a chauffeur, homework-checker and barf-cleaner-upper all rolled into one. She's always there for her kids and ready to jump into action during a crisis, whether it's a fight between the twins or Leni's missing shoe. When she's not chasing the kids around or at her day job as a dental hygienist, Mom pursues her passion: writing. She also loves taking on house projects and is very handy with tools (guess that's where Lana gets it from). Between writing, working and being a mom, her days are always hectic but she wouldn't have it any other way.

LYNN LOUD SR.

Dad (Lynn Loud Sr.) is a fun-loving, upbeat aspiring chef. A kid-at-heart, he's not above taking part in the kids' zany schemes. In addition to cooking, Dad loves his van, playing the cowbell and making puns. Before meeting Mom, Dad spent a semester in England and has been obsessed with British culture ever since – and sometimes "accidentally" slips into a British accent. When Dad's not wrangling the kids, he's pursuing his dream of opening his own restaurant where he hopes to make his "Lynn-sagnas" world-famous.

CLYDE McBRIDE
THE BEST FRIEND (11)

Clyde is Lincoln's partner in crime. He's always willing to go along with Lincoln's crazy schemes (even if he sees the flaws in them up-front). Lincoln and Clyde are two peas in a pod and share pretty much all of the same tastes in movies, comics, TV shows, toys—you name it. As an only child, Clyde envies Lincoln—how cool would it be to always have siblings around to talk to? But since Clyde spends so much time at the Loud household, he's almost an honorary sibling anyway.

ZACH GURDLE

Zach is a self-admitted nerd who's obsessed with aliens and conspiracy theories. He lives between a freeway and a circus, so the chaos of the Loud House doesn't faze him. He and Rusty occasionally butt heads, but deep down, it's all love.

RUSTY SPOKES

Rusty is a self-proclaimed ladies' man who's always the first to dish out girl advice—even though he's never been on an actual date. His dad owns a suit rental service, so occasionally Rusty can hook the gang up with some dapper duds—just as long as no one gets anything dirty.

LIAM

Liam is an enthusiastic, sweet-natured farm boy full of down-home wisdom. He loves hanging out with his Mee Maw, wrestling his prize pig Virginia, and sharing his farm-to-table produce with the rest of the gang.

STELLA

Stella, 11, is a quirky, carefree girl who's new to Royal Woods. She has tons of interests, like trying on wigs, playing laser tag, eating curly fries, and hanging with her friends. But what she loves the most is tech—she always wants to dismantle electronics and put them back together again.

SAM SHARP

Sam, 15, is Luna's class-mate and good friend, who Luna has a crush on. Sam is all about the music – she loves to play guitar and write and compose music. Her favorite genre is rock and roll but she appreciates all good tunes. Unlike Luna, Sam only has one brother, Simon, but she thinks even one sibling provides enough chaos for her.

BOBBY SANTIAGO

Ronnie Anne's older brother, Bobby is a sweet, responsible, loyal high-school senior who works in the family's bodega. Bobby is very devoted to his family. He's Grandpa's right hand man and can't wait to one day take over the bodega for him. Bobby's a big kid and a bit of a klutz, which sometimes gets him into pickles, like locking himself in the freezer case. But he makes up for any work mishaps with his great customer skills – everyone in the neighborhood loves him.

CHUNK

Chunk is Luna's friend and roadie. He's Luna's right-hand man when it comes to lifting equipment and is always there in a pinch when she needs an extra guitar. He's super creative and can turn any discarded appliance into an instrument. When he's not rolling around in his awesome van, you can find him performing as the lead singer and guitarist of "Chunk and the Pieces."

| ROXANNE | CHINAH | CLAUDETTE | JACKIE |

THE PAGEANT QUEENS

LINDSEY SWEETWATER

LENI'S COWORKER FRIENDS

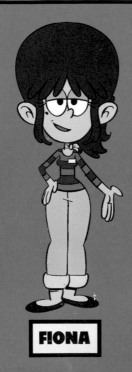

FIONA

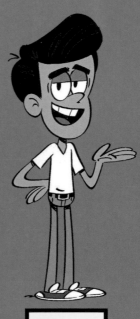

MIGUEL

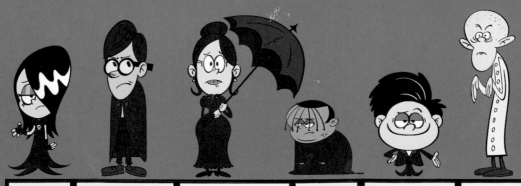

HAIKU	MORPHEUS	PERSEPHONE	DANTE	BERTRAND	BORIS

MORTICIANS CLUB

POP POP

Albert, the Loud kids' grandfather, currently lives at Sunset Canyon Retirement Community after dedicating his life to working in the military. Pop Pop spends his days dominating at shuffleboard, eating pudding and going on adventures with his pals Bernie, Scoots, and Seymour and his girlfriend, Myrtle. Pop Pop is upbeat, fun-loving and cherishes spending time with his grandchildren.

MYRTLE

Myrtle, or Gran-Gran, is Albert's (Pop Pop's) girlfriend. She loves traveling and hanging out with Albert and the Loud kids. Since she doesn't have grandkids of her own, she's the Loud kids' honorary grandma and can't help but smother them with love.

POP POP'S FRIENDS

BERNIE

SCOOTS

SEYMOUR

HAROLD AND HOWARD McBRIDE
Clyde's Loving Dads

Harold and Howard are Clyde's loving dads and only want the best for him, but what they define as "the best" may differ. Harold is a level-headed, straight-shooter with a heart of gold. The more easygoing of Clyde's dads, Harold often has to convince Howard that it's okay for them to not constantly hover over Clyde. Howard is an anxious helicopter parent and it's easy for him to break down into emotional sobbing, whether it be sad times (like when Clyde stubbed his toe) or happy (like when Clyde and Lincoln beat that really tough video game boss). Despite their differing parenting styles, the two dads bring nothing but love to the table.

FLIP

The owner of Flip's Food & Fuel, the local convenience store. Flip has questionable business practices – he's been known to sell expired milk and stick his feet in the nacho cheese! When he's not selling Flippees, Flip loves fishing and also sponsors Lynn's rec basketball team.

MOLLY WETTA
the Librarian

Molly is a hip, fun, librarian who knows all the kids in town and what they like to read. Molly's one nemesis is Lisa Loud, who owes the library a lot of money in fines for overdue books!

"BUCKLE UP"

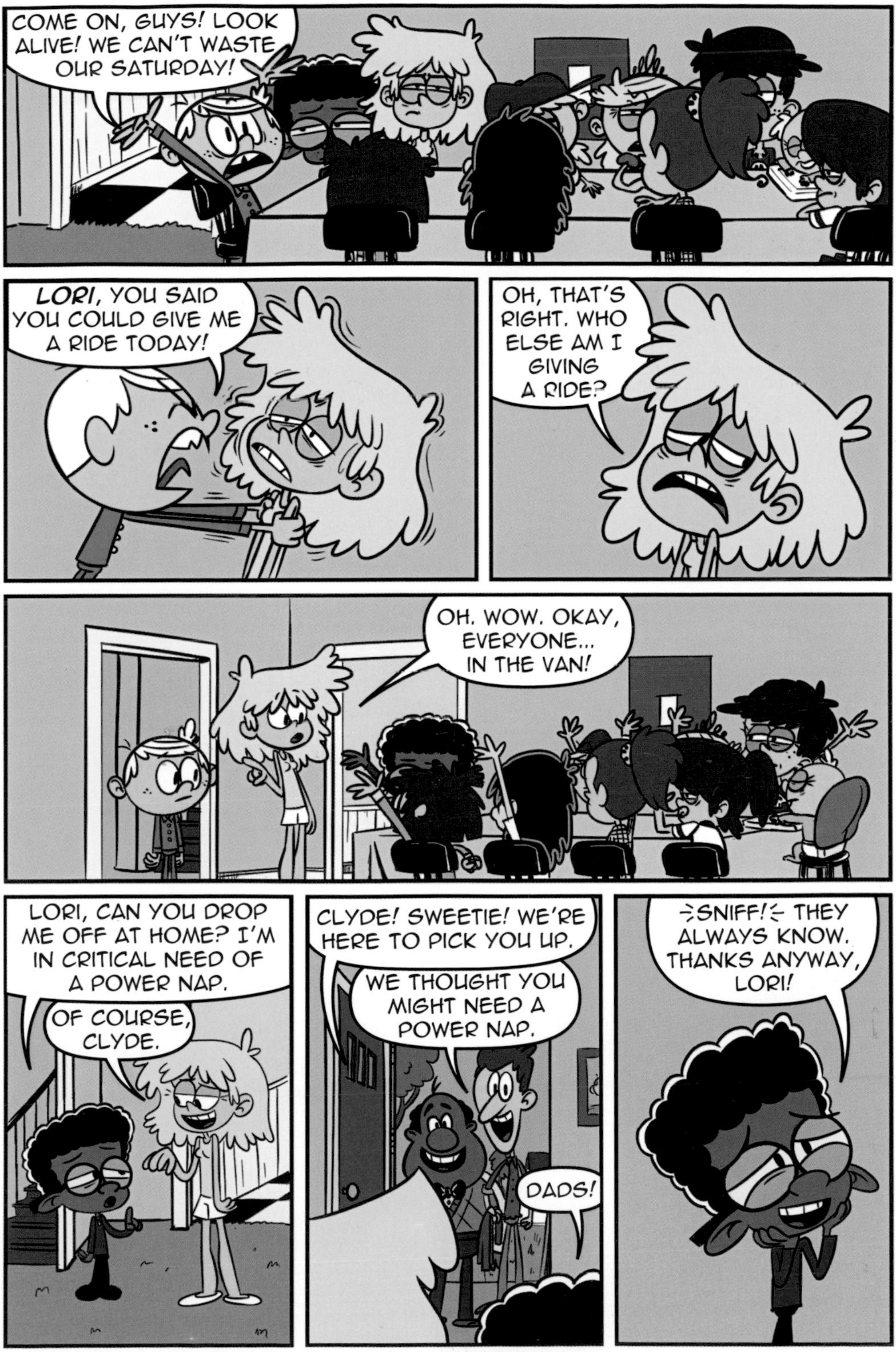
COME ON, GUYS! LOOK ALIVE! WE CAN'T WASTE OUR SATURDAY!
LORI, YOU SAID YOU COULD GIVE ME A RIDE TODAY!
OH, THAT'S RIGHT. WHO ELSE AM I GIVING A RIDE?
OH. WOW. OKAY, EVERYONE... IN THE VAN!
LORI, CAN YOU DROP ME OFF AT HOME? I'M IN CRITICAL NEED OF A POWER NAP.
OF COURSE, CLYDE.
CLYDE! SWEETIE! WE'RE HERE TO PICK YOU UP.
WE THOUGHT YOU MIGHT NEED A POWER NAP.
DADS!
SNIFF! THEY ALWAYS KNOW. THANKS ANYWAY, LORI!

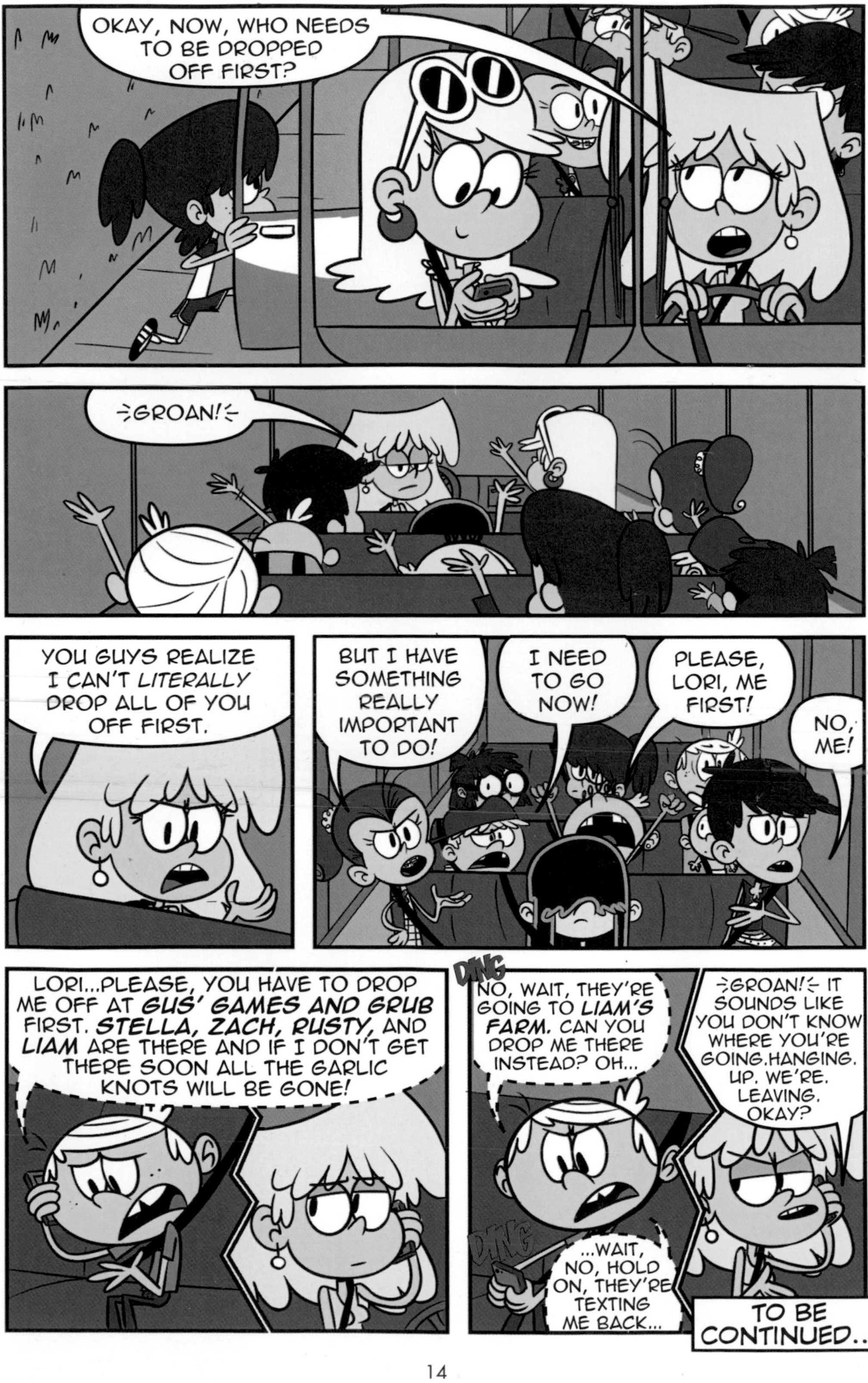
OKAY, NOW, WHO NEEDS TO BE DROPPED OFF FIRST?
GROAN!
YOU GUYS REALIZE I CAN'T *LITERALLY* DROP ALL OF YOU OFF FIRST.
BUT I HAVE SOMETHING REALLY IMPORTANT TO DO!
I NEED TO GO NOW!
PLEASE, LORI, ME FIRST!
NO, ME!
LORI...PLEASE, YOU HAVE TO DROP ME OFF AT ***GUS' GAMES AND GRUB*** FIRST. ***STELLA, ZACH, RUSTY,*** AND ***LIAM*** ARE THERE AND IF I DON'T GET THERE SOON ALL THE GARLIC KNOTS WILL BE GONE!
DING
NO, WAIT, THEY'RE GOING TO ***LIAM'S FARM.*** CAN YOU DROP ME THERE INSTEAD? OH...
DING
...WAIT, NO, HOLD ON, THEY'RE TEXTING ME BACK...
GROAN! IT SOUNDS LIKE YOU DON'T KNOW WHERE YOU'RE GOING.HANGING. UP. WE'RE. LEAVING. OKAY?
TO BE CONTINUED...

"MALL FLOP"

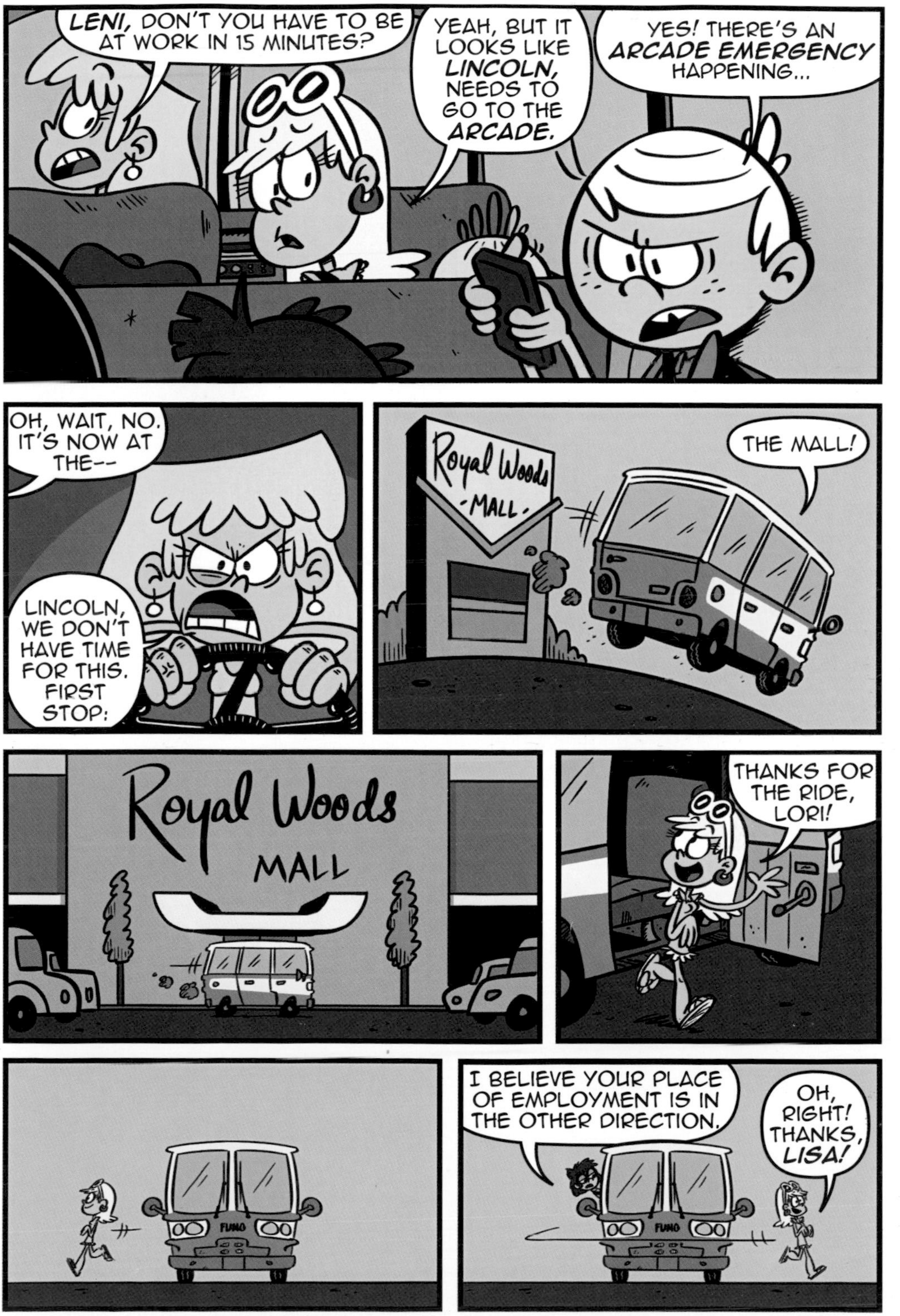
LENI, DON'T YOU HAVE TO BE AT WORK IN 15 MINUTES?
YEAH, BUT IT LOOKS LIKE LINCOLN, NEEDS TO GO TO THE ARCADE.
YES! THERE'S AN ARCADE EMERGENCY HAPPENING...
OH, WAIT, NO. IT'S NOW AT THE--
LINCOLN, WE DON'T HAVE TIME FOR THIS. FIRST STOP:
Royal Woods MALL
THE MALL!
Royal Woods MALL
THANKS FOR THE RIDE, LORI!
I BELIEVE YOUR PLACE OF EMPLOYMENT IS IN THE OTHER DIRECTION.
OH, RIGHT! THANKS, LISA!

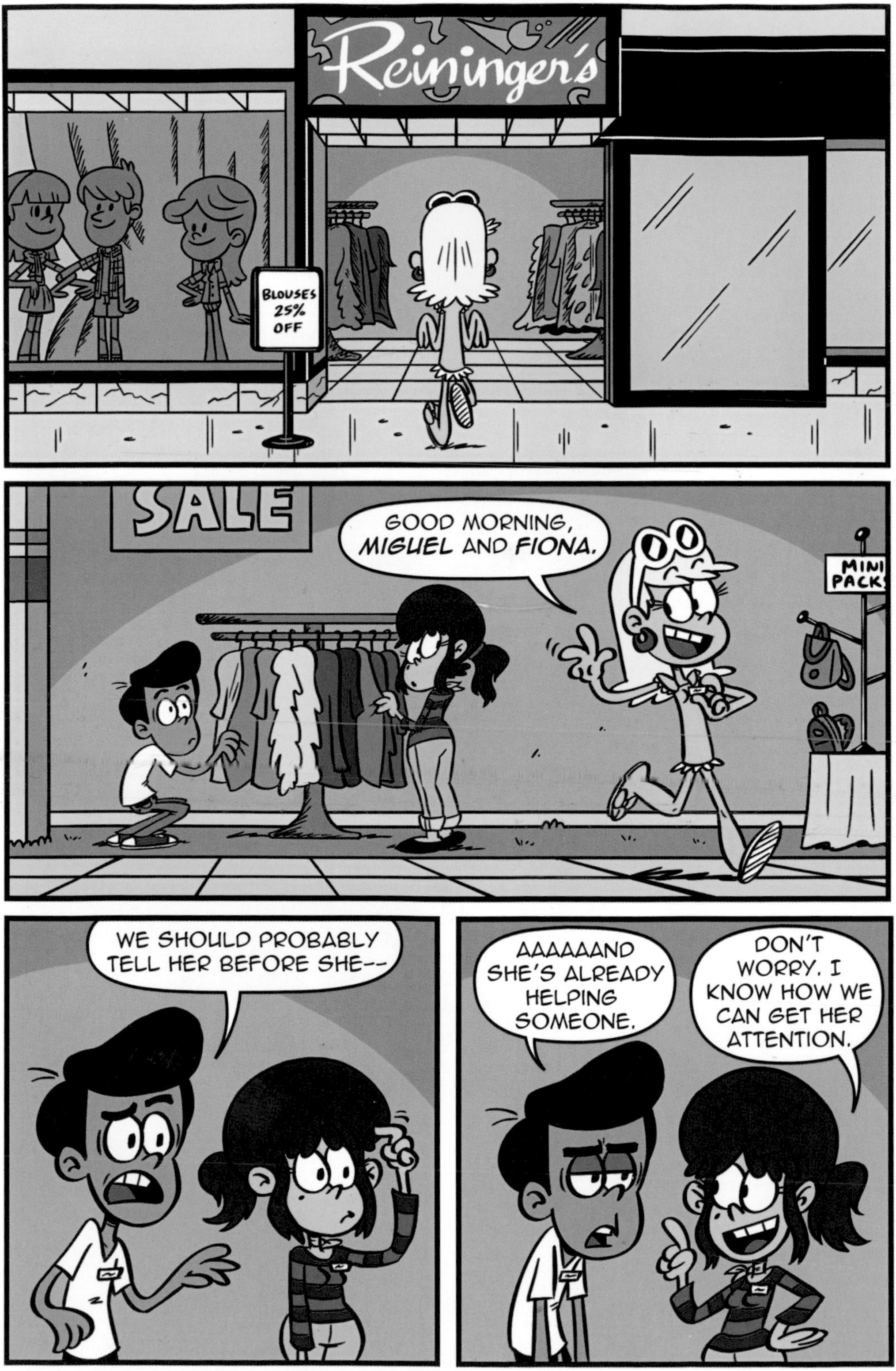
Reininger's
BLOUSES 25% OFF
SALE
GOOD MORNING, MIGUEL AND FIONA.
MINI PACKS
WE SHOULD PROBABLY TELL HER BEFORE SHE--
AAAAAAND SHE'S ALREADY HELPING SOMEONE.
DON'T WORRY. I KNOW HOW WE CAN GET HER ATTENTION.

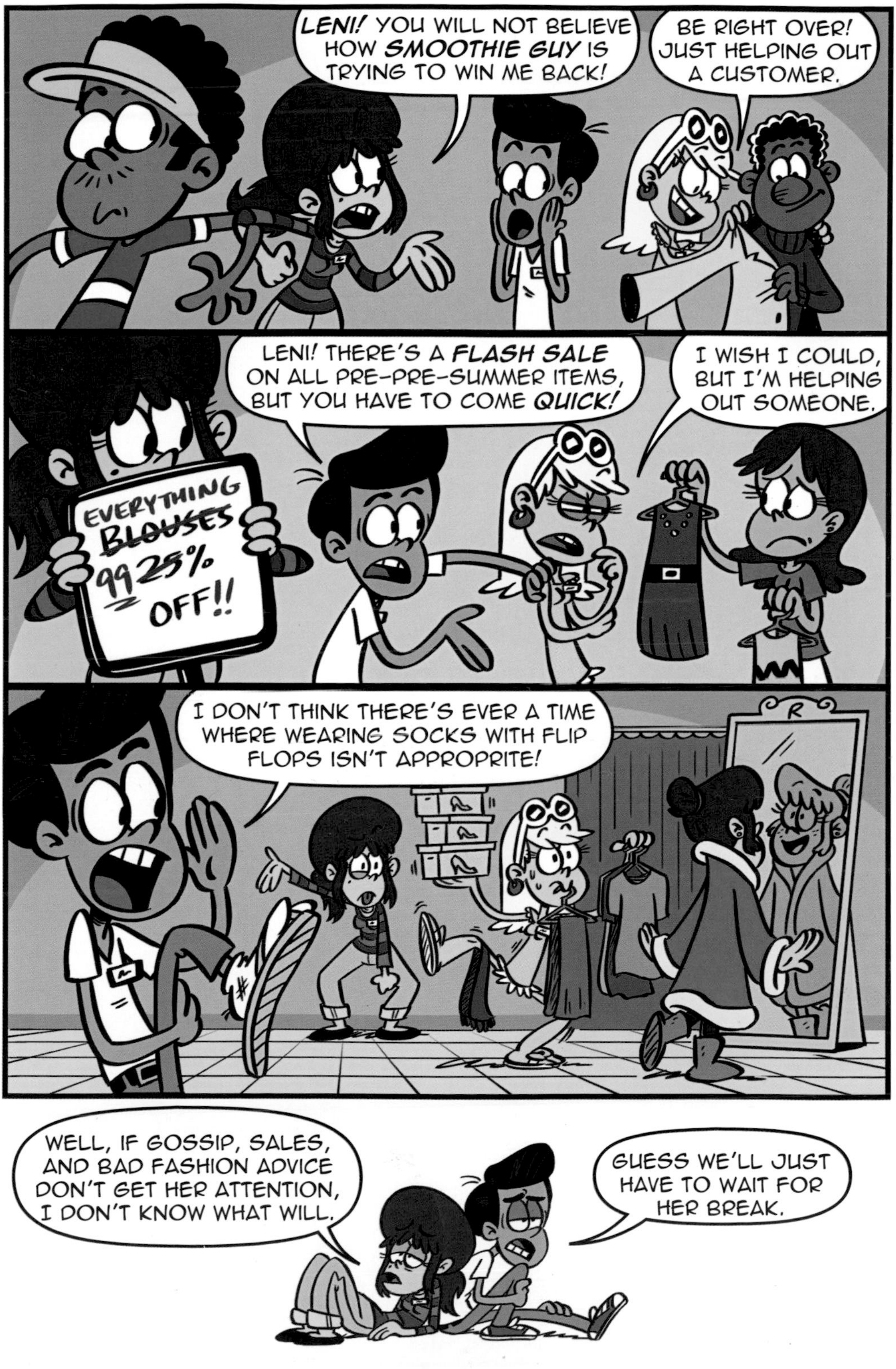
LENI! YOU WILL NOT BELIEVE HOW SMOOTHIE GUY IS TRYING TO WIN ME BACK!
BE RIGHT OVER! JUST HELPING OUT A CUSTOMER.
EVERYTHING BLOUSES 99 25% OFF!!
LENI! THERE'S A FLASH SALE ON ALL PRE-PRE-SUMMER ITEMS, BUT YOU HAVE TO COME QUICK!
I WISH I COULD, BUT I'M HELPING OUT SOMEONE.
I DON'T THINK THERE'S EVER A TIME WHERE WEARING SOCKS WITH FLIP FLOPS ISN'T APPROPRITE!
R
WELL, IF GOSSIP, SALES, AND BAD FASHION ADVICE DON'T GET HER ATTENTION, I DON'T KNOW WHAT WILL.
GUESS WE'LL JUST HAVE TO WAIT FOR HER BREAK.

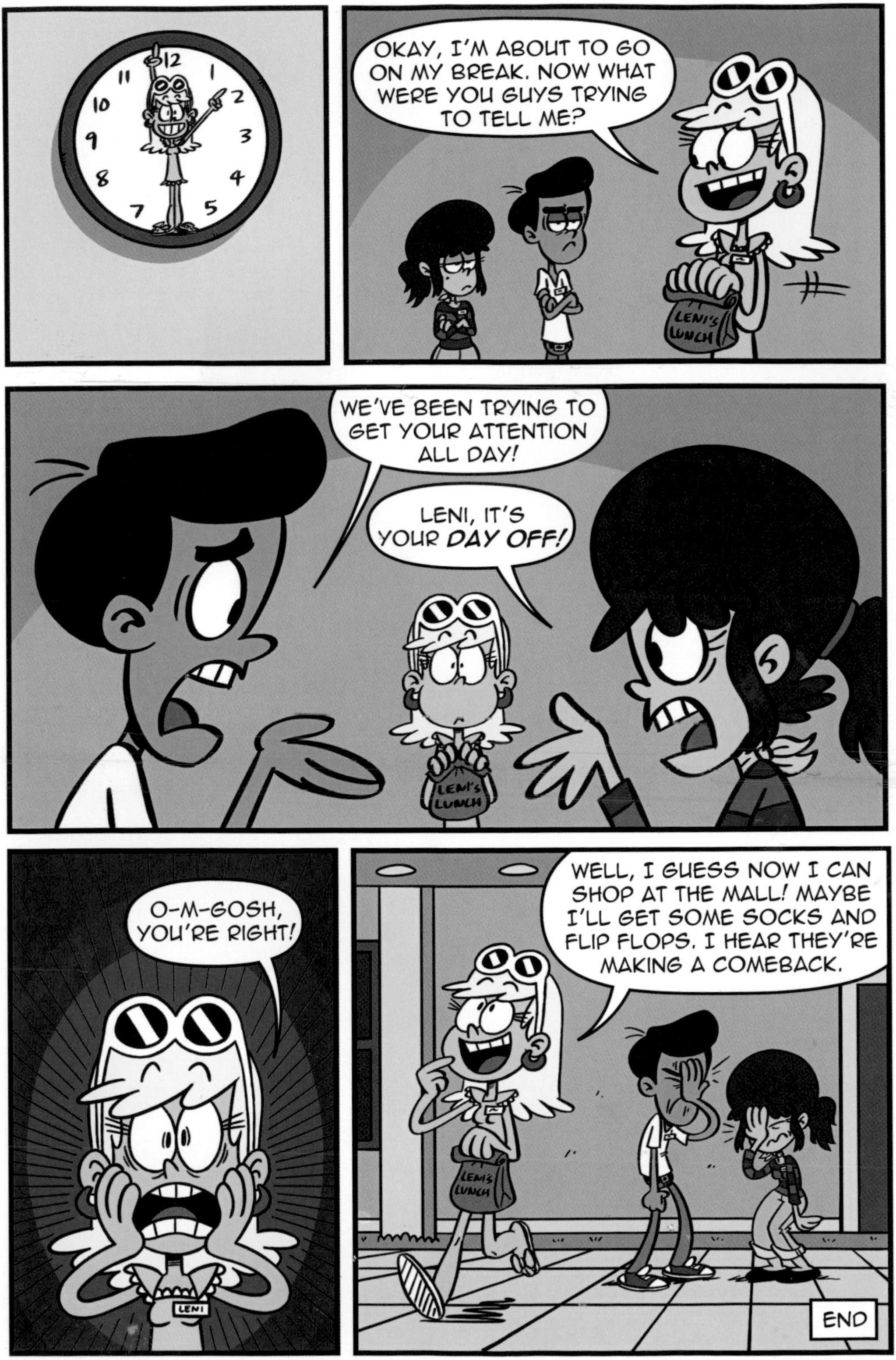
12
1
2
3
4
5
7
8
9
10
11
OKAY, I'M ABOUT TO GO ON MY BREAK. NOW WHAT WERE YOU GUYS TRYING TO TELL ME?
LENI'S LUNCH
WE'VE BEEN TRYING TO GET YOUR ATTENTION ALL DAY!
LENI, IT'S YOUR ***DAY OFF!***
LENI'S LUNCH
O-M-GOSH, YOU'RE RIGHT!
LENI
WELL, I GUESS NOW I CAN SHOP AT THE MALL! MAYBE I'LL GET SOME SOCKS AND FLIP FLOPS. I HEAR THEY'RE MAKING A COMEBACK.
LENI'S LUNCH
END

"BANDS ON THE RUN"

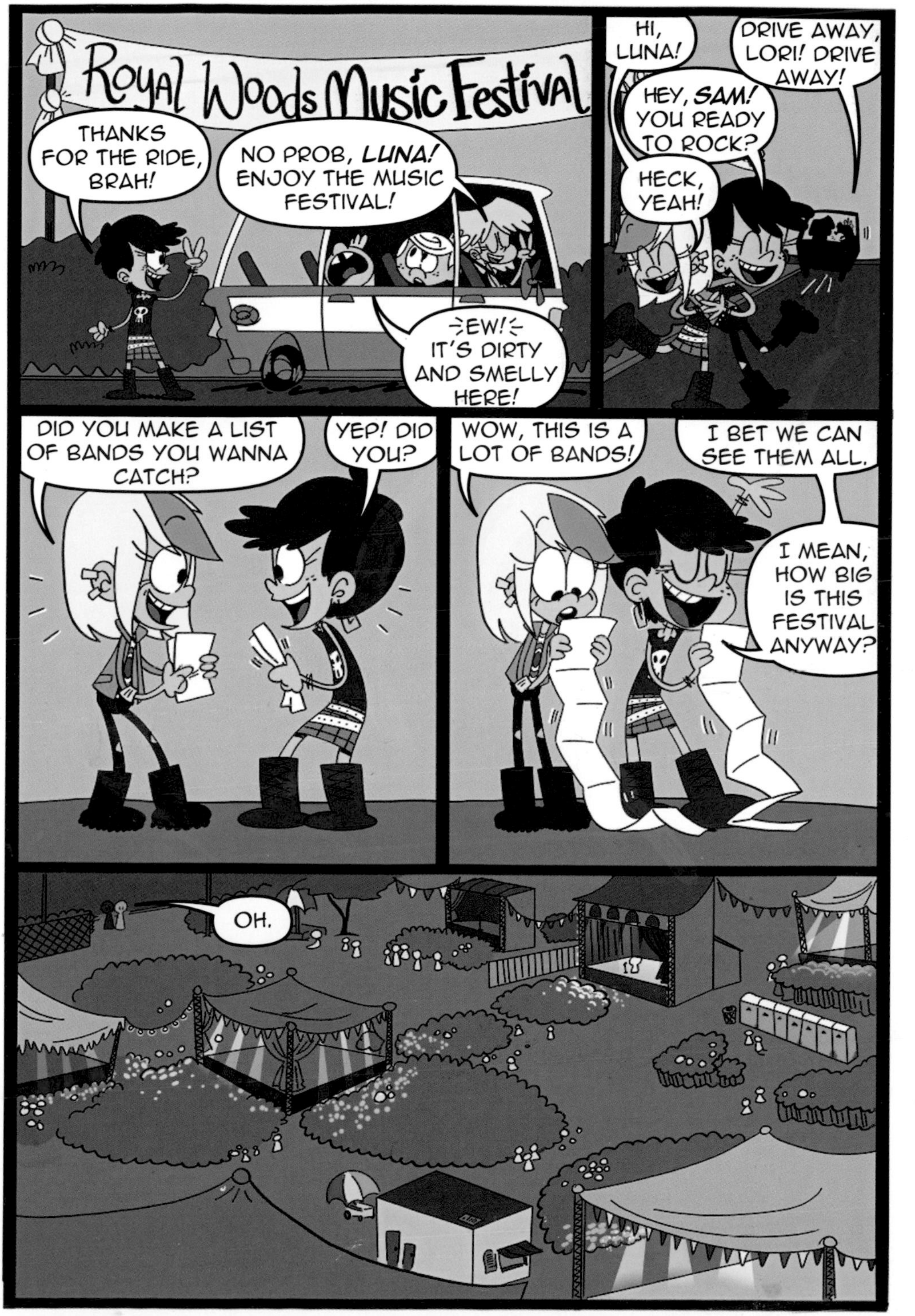
Royal Woods Music Festival
THANKS FOR THE RIDE, BRAH!
NO PROB, LUNA! ENJOY THE MUSIC FESTIVAL!
EW! IT'S DIRTY AND SMELLY HERE!
HI, LUNA!
HEY, SAM! YOU READY TO ROCK?
HECK, YEAH!
DRIVE AWAY, LORI! DRIVE AWAY!
DID YOU MAKE A LIST OF BANDS YOU WANNA CATCH?
YEP! DID YOU?
WOW, THIS IS A LOT OF BANDS!
I BET WE CAN SEE THEM ALL.
I MEAN, HOW BIG IS THIS FESTIVAL ANYWAY?
OH.

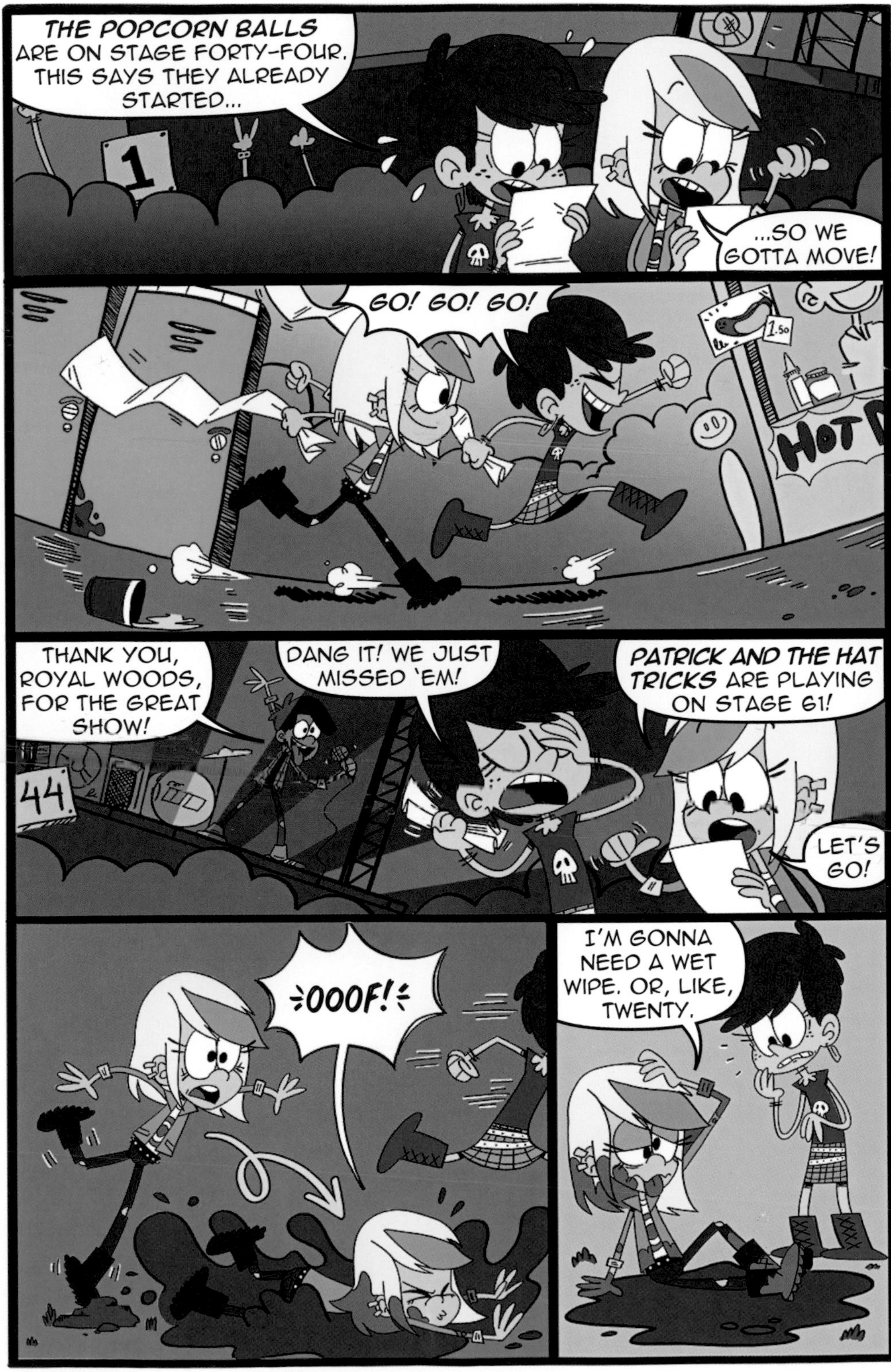
THE POPCORN BALLS ARE ON STAGE FORTY-FOUR. THIS SAYS THEY ALREADY STARTED...
...SO WE GOTTA MOVE!
GO! GO! GO!
1.50
HOT D
THANK YOU, ROYAL WOODS, FOR THE GREAT SHOW!
DANG IT! WE JUST MISSED 'EM!
PATRICK AND THE HAT TRICKS ARE PLAYING ON STAGE 61!
LET'S GO!
44
OOOF!
I'M GONNA NEED A WET WIPE. OR, LIKE, TWENTY.

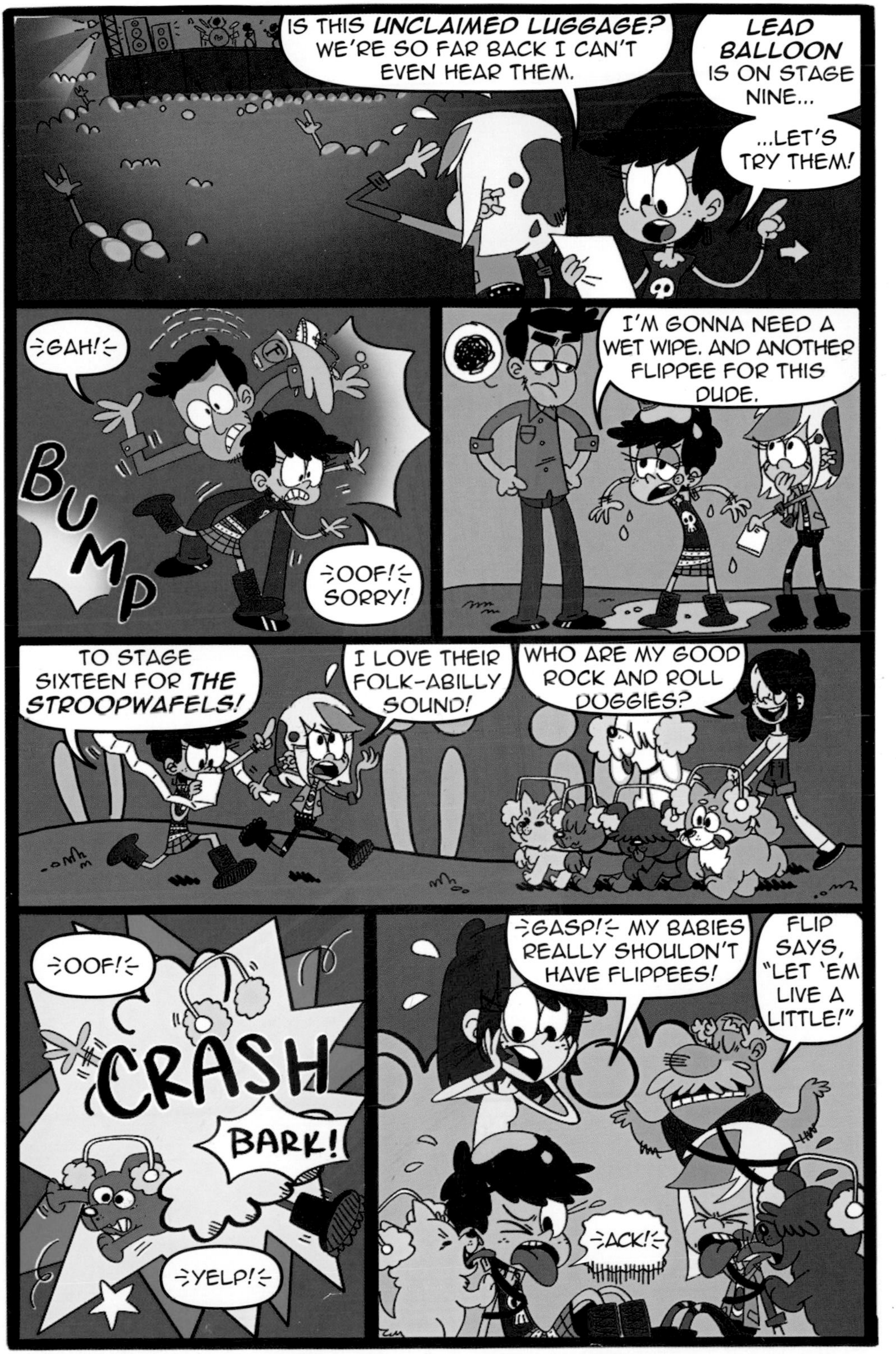
IS THIS UNCLAIMED LUGGAGE? WE'RE SO FAR BACK I CAN'T EVEN HEAR THEM.
LEAD BALLOON IS ON STAGE NINE...
...LET'S TRY THEM!
GAH!
BUMP
OOF! SORRY!
I'M GONNA NEED A WET WIPE. AND ANOTHER FLIPPEE FOR THIS DUDE.
TO STAGE SIXTEEN FOR THE STROOPWAFELS!
I LOVE THEIR FOLK-ABILLY SOUND!
WHO ARE MY GOOD ROCK AND ROLL DOGGIES?
OOF!
CRASH
BARK!
YELP!
GASP! MY BABIES REALLY SHOULDN'T HAVE FLIPPEES!
FLIP SAYS, "LET 'EM LIVE A LITTLE!"
ACK!

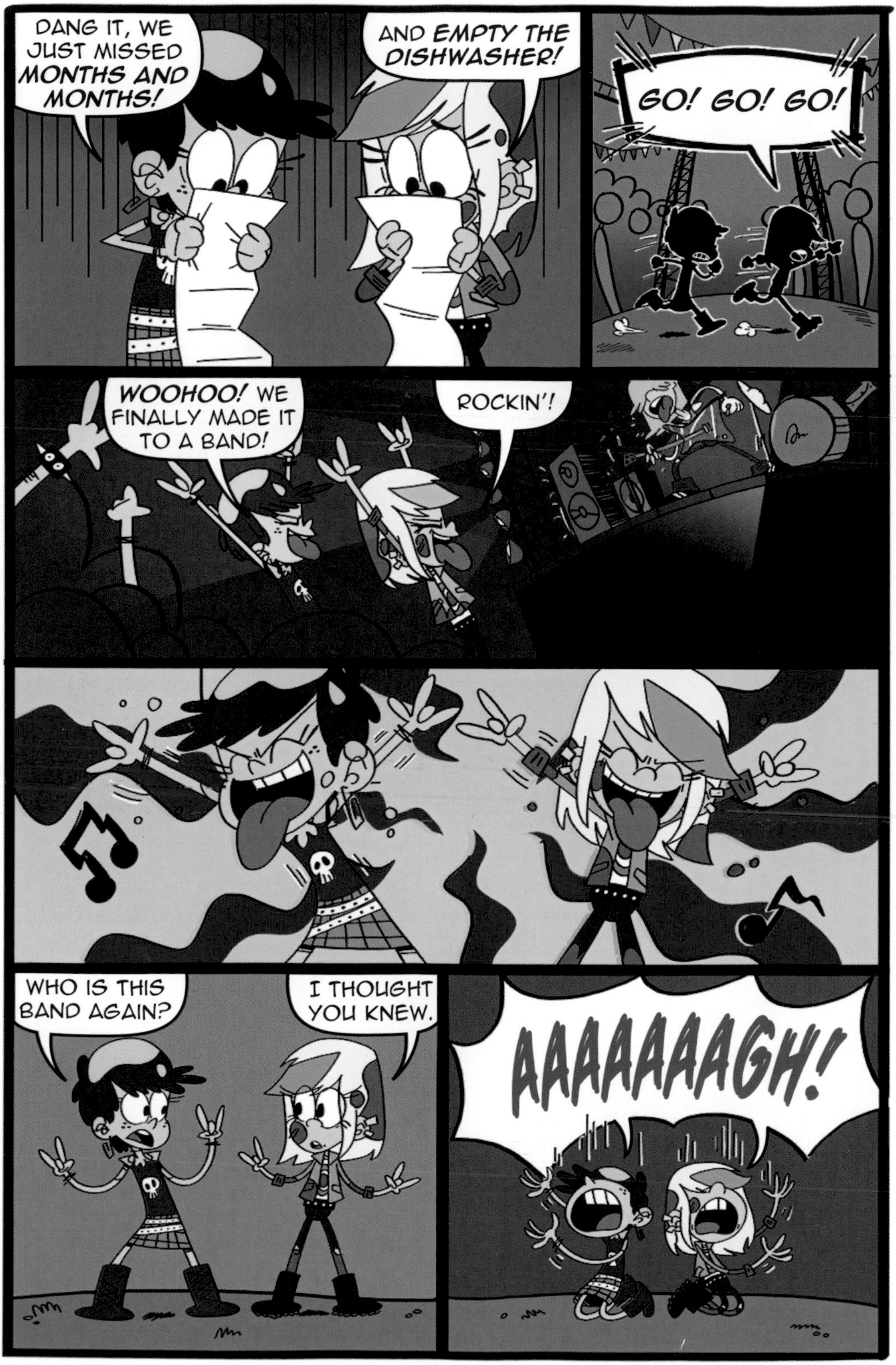
DANG IT, WE JUST MISSED MONTHS AND MONTHS!
AND EMPTY THE DISHWASHER!
GO! GO! GO!
WOOHOO! WE FINALLY MADE IT TO A BAND!
ROCKIN'!
WHO IS THIS BAND AGAIN?
I THOUGHT YOU KNEW.
AAAAAAAGH!

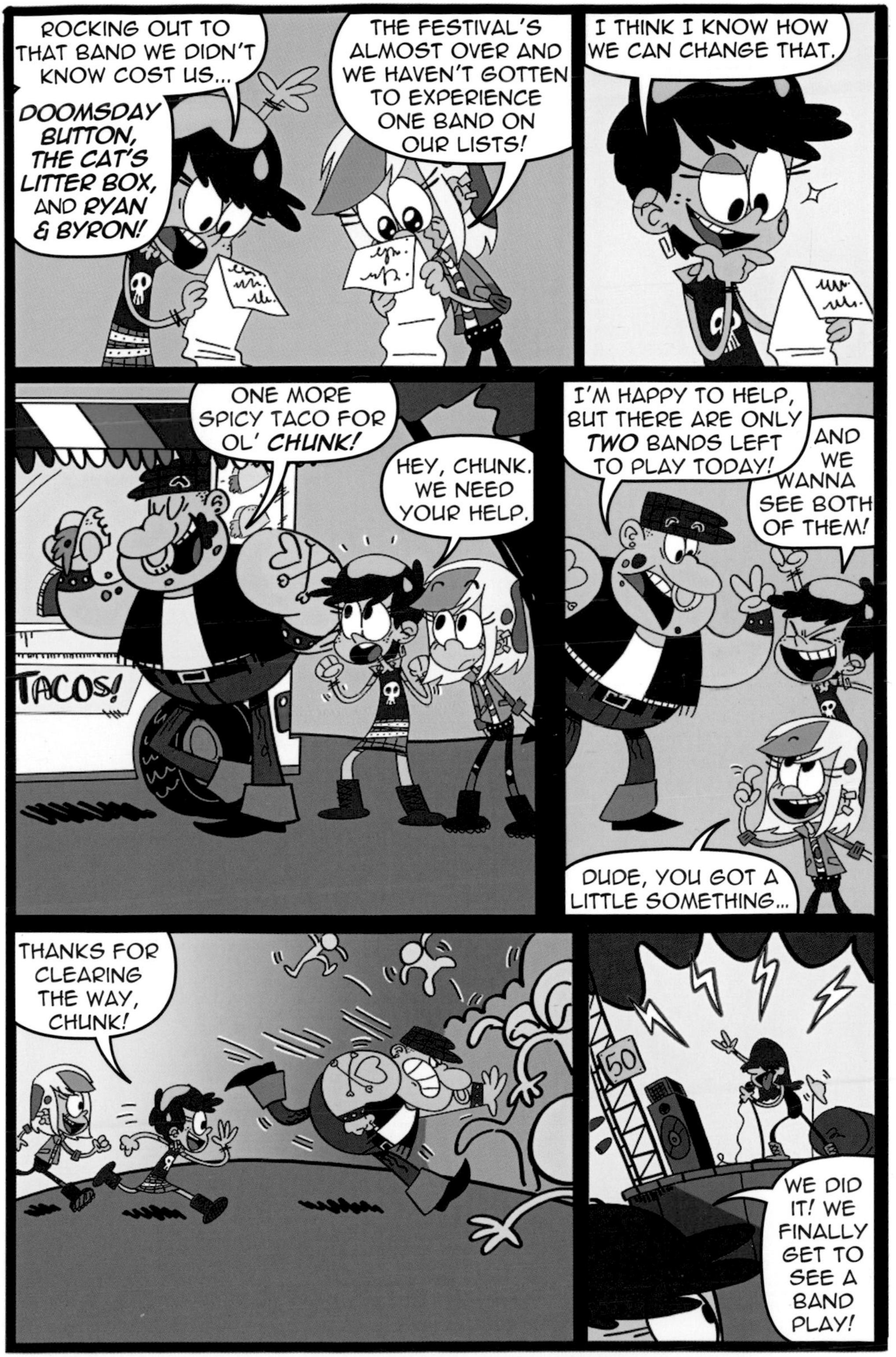
ROCKING OUT TO THAT BAND WE DIDN'T KNOW COST US...
DOOMSDAY BUTTON, THE CAT'S LITTER BOX, AND RYAN & BYRON!
THE FESTIVAL'S ALMOST OVER AND WE HAVEN'T GOTTEN TO EXPERIENCE ONE BAND ON OUR LISTS!
I THINK I KNOW HOW WE CAN CHANGE THAT.
ONE MORE SPICY TACO FOR OL' CHUNK!
TACOS!
HEY, CHUNK. WE NEED YOUR HELP.
I'M HAPPY TO HELP, BUT THERE ARE ONLY TWO BANDS LEFT TO PLAY TODAY!
AND WE WANNA SEE BOTH OF THEM!
DUDE, YOU GOT A LITTLE SOMETHING...
THANKS FOR CLEARING THE WAY, CHUNK!
50
WE DID IT! WE FINALLY GET TO SEE A BAND PLAY!

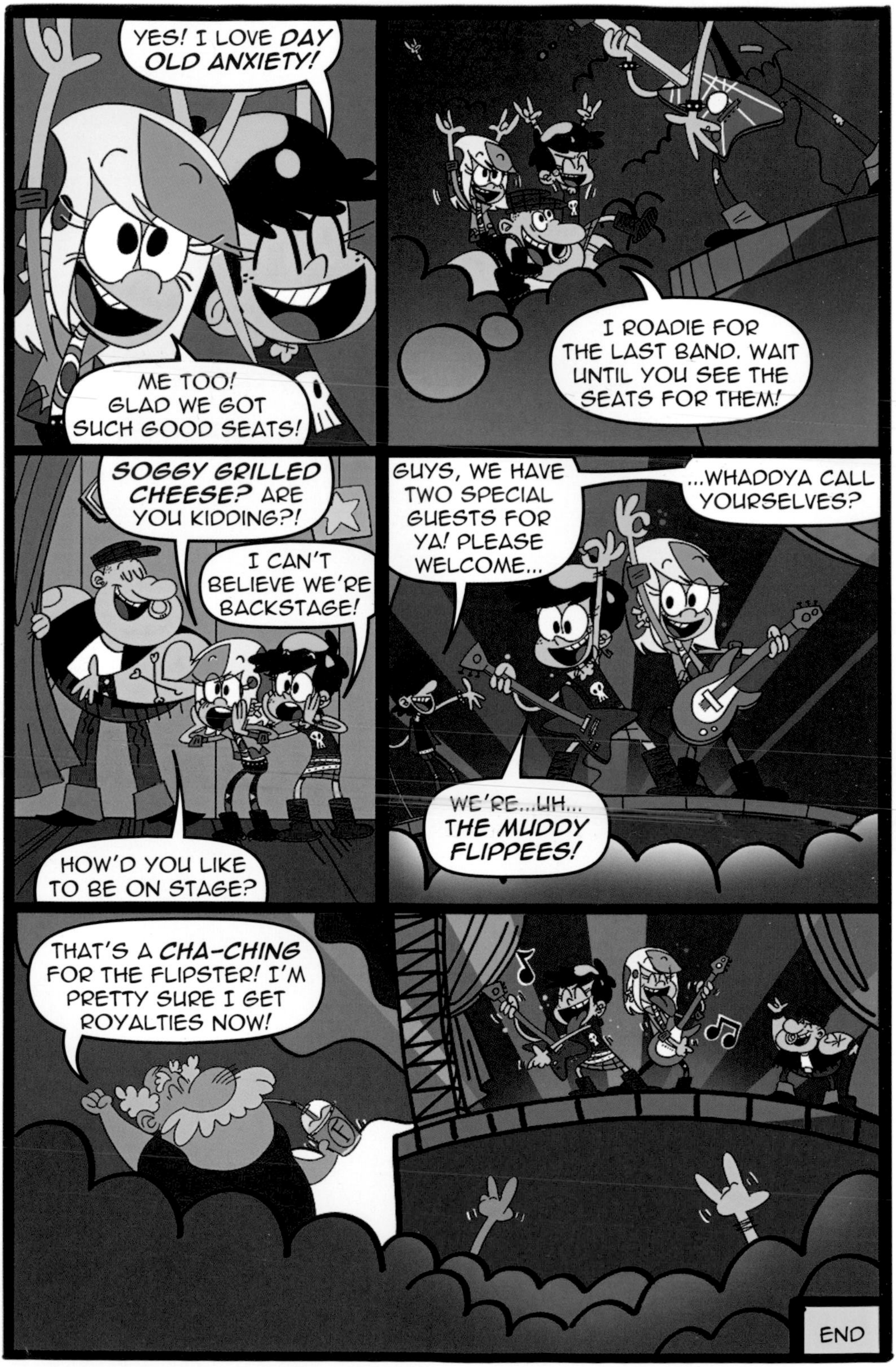

YES! I LOVE DAY OLD ANXIETY!
ME TOO! GLAD WE GOT SUCH GOOD SEATS!
I ROADIE FOR THE LAST BAND. WAIT UNTIL YOU SEE THE SEATS FOR THEM!
SOGGY GRILLED CHEESE? ARE YOU KIDDING?!
I CAN'T BELIEVE WE'RE BACKSTAGE!
HOW'D YOU LIKE TO BE ON STAGE?
GUYS, WE HAVE TWO SPECIAL GUESTS FOR YA! PLEASE WELCOME...
...WHADDYA CALL YOURSELVES?
WE'RE...UH... THE MUDDY FLIPPEES!
THAT'S A CHA-CHING FOR THE FLIPSTER! I'M PRETTY SURE I GET ROYALTIES NOW!
END

"THE PAGEANT TRAP"

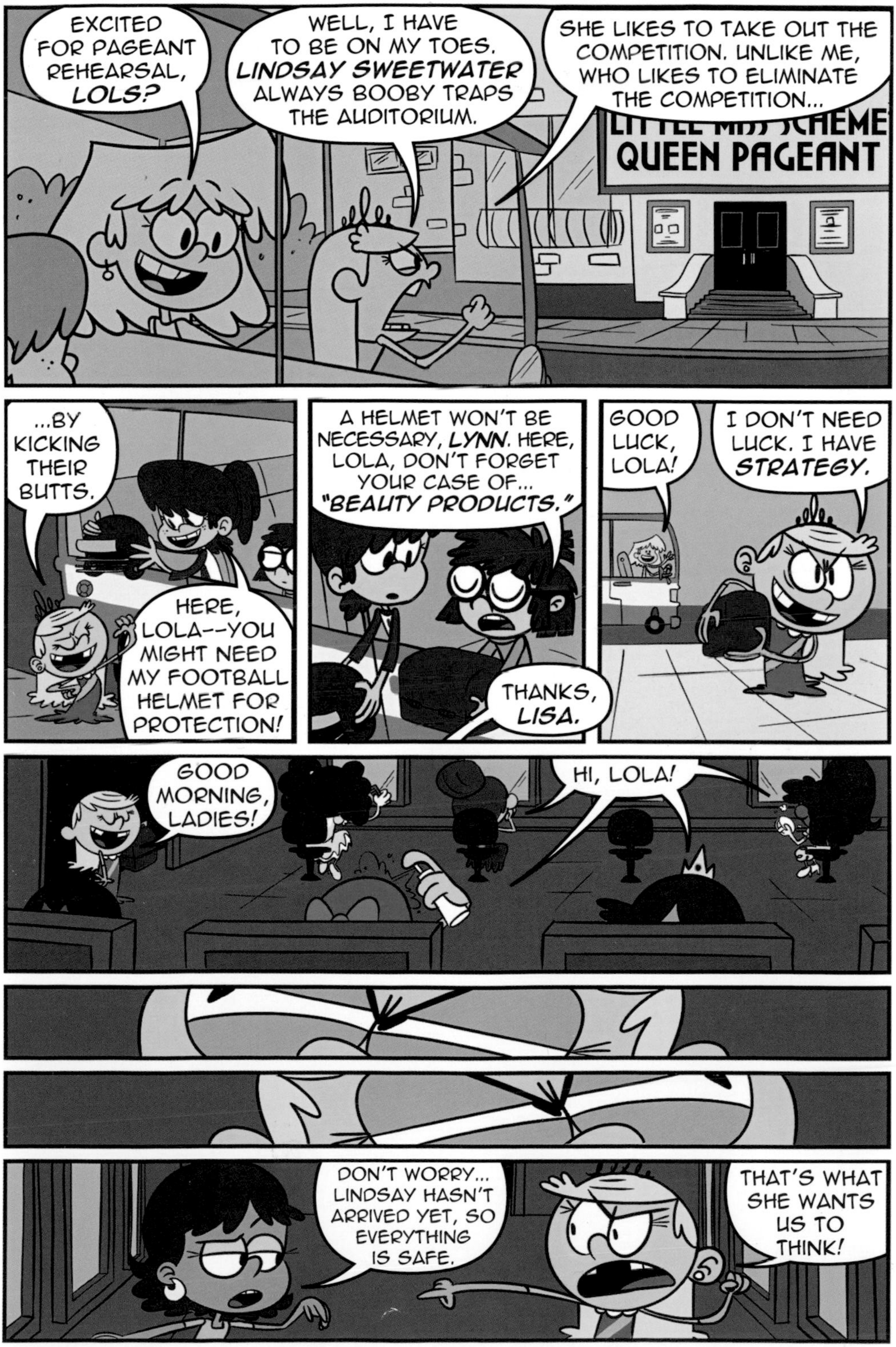
EXCITED FOR PAGEANT REHEARSAL, LOLS?
WELL, I HAVE TO BE ON MY TOES. LINDSAY SWEETWATER ALWAYS BOOBY TRAPS THE AUDITORIUM.
SHE LIKES TO TAKE OUT THE COMPETITION. UNLIKE ME, WHO LIKES TO ELIMINATE THE COMPETITION...
LITTLE MISS SCHEME QUEEN PAGEANT
...BY KICKING THEIR BUTTS.
HERE, LOLA--YOU MIGHT NEED MY FOOTBALL HELMET FOR PROTECTION!
A HELMET WON'T BE NECESSARY, LYNN. HERE, LOLA, DON'T FORGET YOUR CASE OF... "BEAUTY PRODUCTS."
THANKS, LISA.
GOOD LUCK, LOLA!
I DON'T NEED LUCK. I HAVE STRATEGY.
GOOD MORNING, LADIES!
HI, LOLA!
DON'T WORRY... LINDSAY HASN'T ARRIVED YET, SO EVERYTHING IS SAFE.
THAT'S WHAT SHE WANTS US TO THINK!

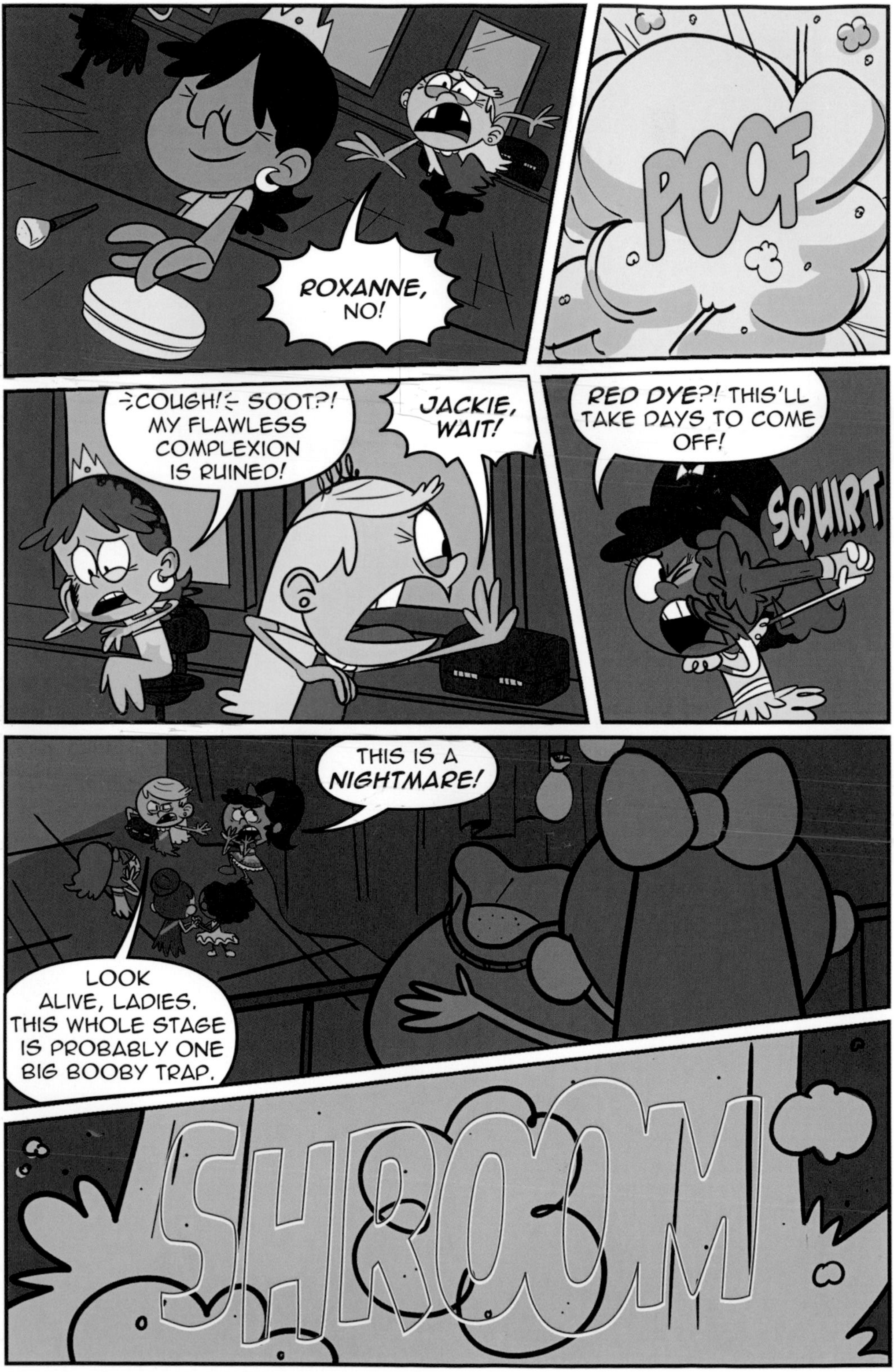
ROXANNE, NO!
POOF
-COUGH!- SOOT?! MY FLAWLESS COMPLEXION IS RUINED!
JACKIE, WAIT!
RED DYE?! THIS'LL TAKE DAYS TO COME OFF!
SQUIRT
THIS IS A NIGHTMARE!
LOOK ALIVE, LADIES. THIS WHOLE STAGE IS PROBABLY ONE BIG BOOBY TRAP.
SHROOM

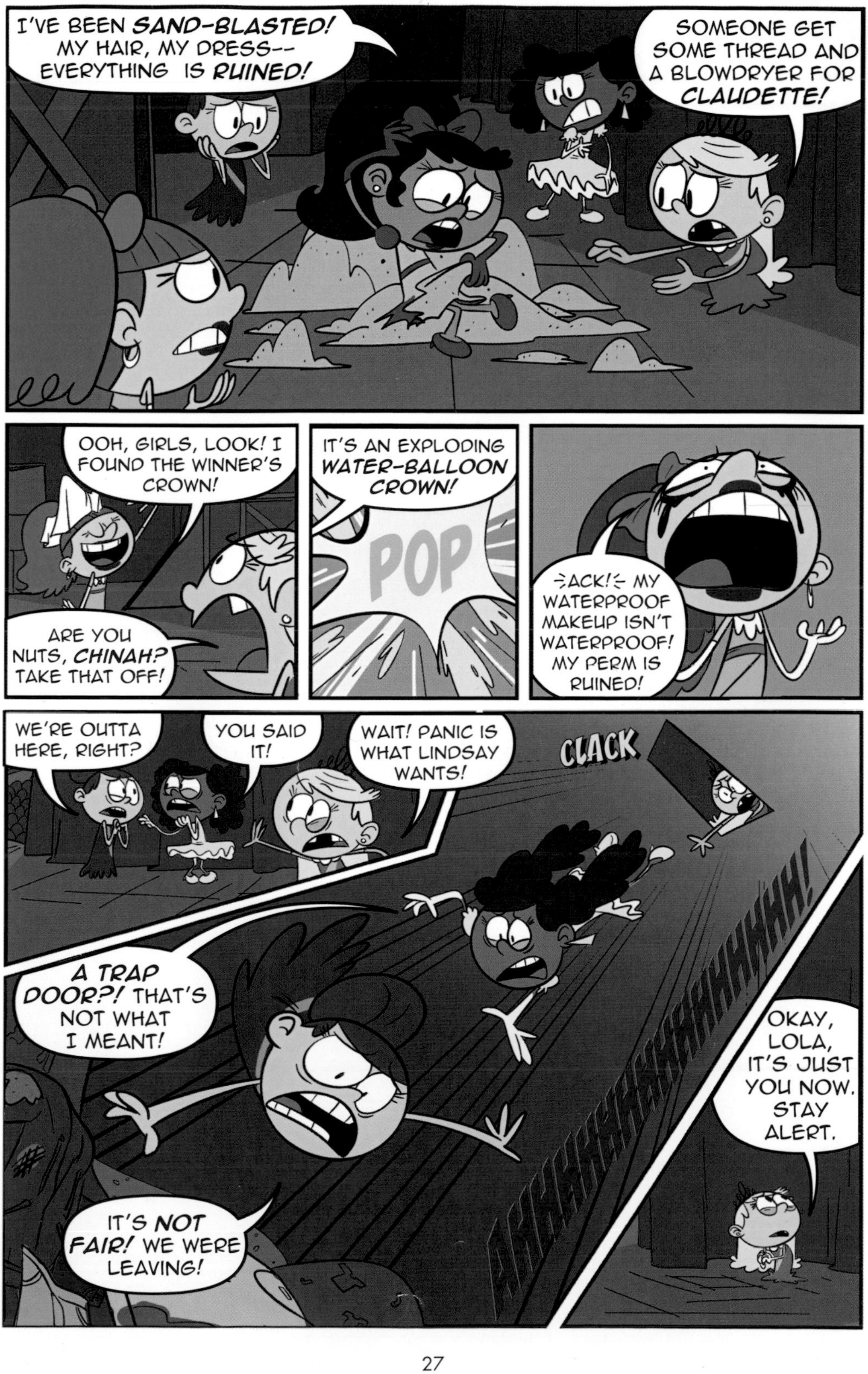
I'VE BEEN SAND-BLASTED! MY HAIR, MY DRESS-- EVERYTHING IS RUINED!
SOMEONE GET SOME THREAD AND A BLOWDRYER FOR CLAUDETTE!
OOH, GIRLS, LOOK! I FOUND THE WINNER'S CROWN!
ARE YOU NUTS, CHINAH? TAKE THAT OFF!
IT'S AN EXPLODING WATER-BALLOON CROWN!
POP
ACK! MY WATERPROOF MAKEUP ISN'T WATERPROOF! MY PERM IS RUINED!
WE'RE OUTTA HERE, RIGHT?
YOU SAID IT!
WAIT! PANIC IS WHAT LINDSAY WANTS!
CLACK
A TRAP DOOR?! THAT'S NOT WHAT I MEANT!
AHHHHHHHHHHHHHHH!
OKAY, LOLA, IT'S JUST YOU NOW. STAY ALERT.
IT'S NOT FAIR! WE WERE LEAVING!

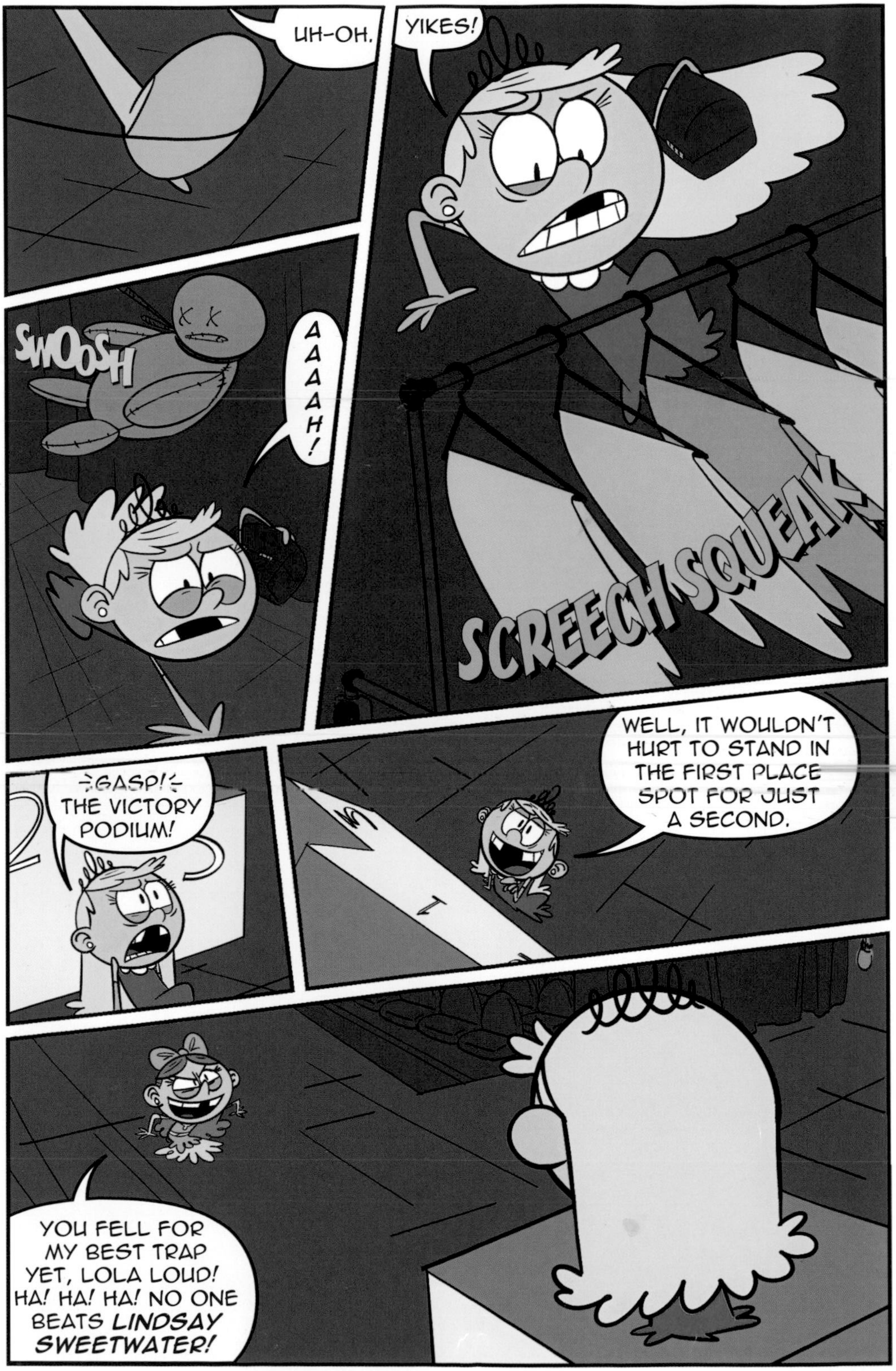
UH-OH.
YIKES!
SWOOSH
AAAAH!
SCREECH SQUEAK
GASP! THE VICTORY PODIUM!
WELL, IT WOULDN'T HURT TO STAND IN THE FIRST PLACE SPOT FOR JUST A SECOND.
YOU FELL FOR MY BEST TRAP YET, LOLA LOUD! HA! HA! HA! NO ONE BEATS LINDSAY SWEETWATER!

WAIT, WHAT'S GOING ON?

GLITCH

A HOLOGRAM?!

1

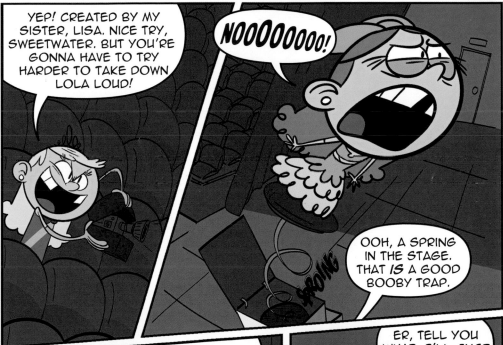

YEP! CREATED BY MY SISTER, LISA. NICE TRY, SWEETWATER. BUT YOU'RE GONNA HAVE TO TRY HARDER TO TAKE DOWN LOLA LOUD!

NOOOOOOOO!

OOH, A SPRING IN THE STAGE. THAT *IS* A GOOD BOOBY TRAP.

SPROING

CONGRATULATIONS TO THIS YEAR'S WINNER...AND, ER, ONLY CONTESTANT, LOLA LOUD! TELL US, TO WHAT DO YOU OWE YOUR VICTORY?

IT'S ALL ABOUT STAYING ONE STEP AHEAD OF THE COMPETITION!

ER, TELL YOU WHAT...I'LL JUST HOLD THAT.

END

"HURRY UP AND WAIT"

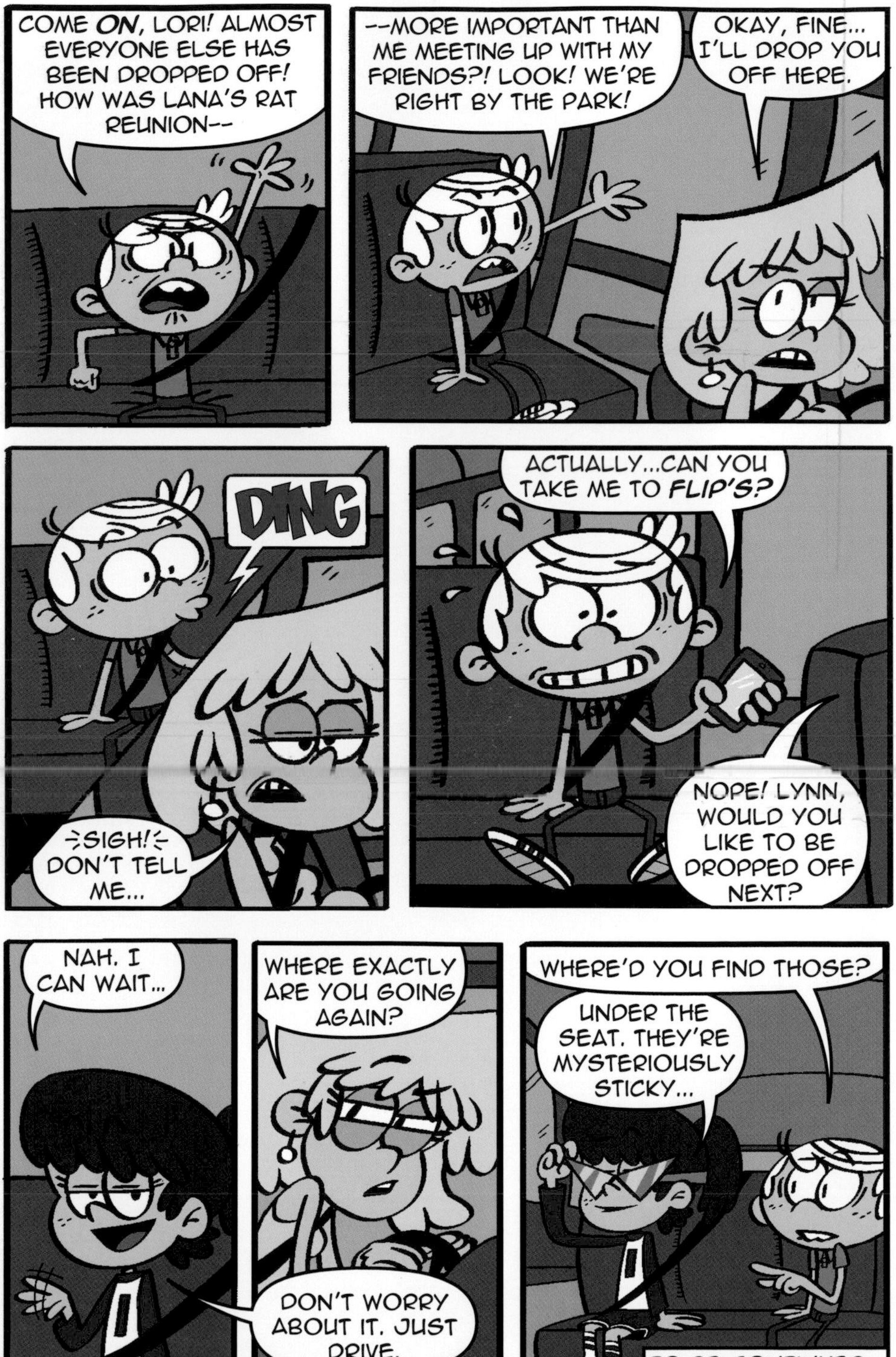

COME ON, LORI! ALMOST EVERYONE ELSE HAS BEEN DROPPED OFF! HOW WAS LANA'S RAT REUNION--
--MORE IMPORTANT THAN ME MEETING UP WITH MY FRIENDS?! LOOK! WE'RE RIGHT BY THE PARK!
OKAY, FINE... I'LL DROP YOU OFF HERE.
DING
-SIGH!- DON'T TELL ME...
ACTUALLY...CAN YOU TAKE ME TO FLIP'S?
NOPE! LYNN, WOULD YOU LIKE TO BE DROPPED OFF NEXT?
NAH. I CAN WAIT...
WHERE EXACTLY ARE YOU GOING AGAIN?
DON'T WORRY ABOUT IT. JUST DRIVE.
WHERE'D YOU FIND THOSE?
UNDER THE SEAT. THEY'RE MYSTERIOUSLY STICKY...
TO BE CONTINUED...

"STAGE FRIGHT"

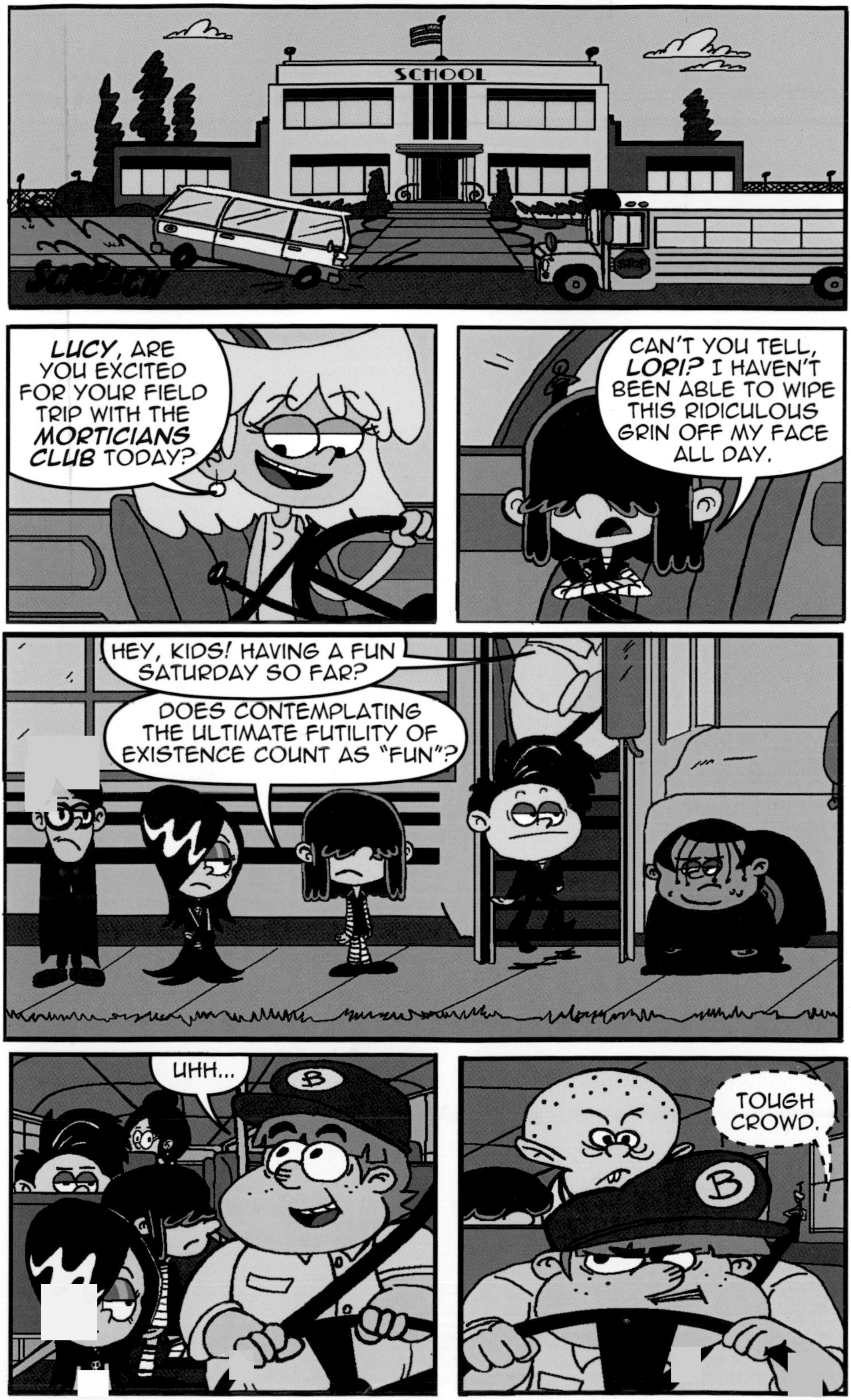
SCHOOL
SCREECH
LUCY, ARE YOU EXCITED FOR YOUR FIELD TRIP WITH THE MORTICIANS CLUB TODAY?
CAN'T YOU TELL, LORI? I HAVEN'T BEEN ABLE TO WIPE THIS RIDICULOUS GRIN OFF MY FACE ALL DAY.
HEY, KIDS! HAVING A FUN SATURDAY SO FAR?
DOES CONTEMPLATING THE ULTIMATE FUTILITY OF EXISTENCE COUNT AS "FUN"?
UHH...
TOUGH CROWD.

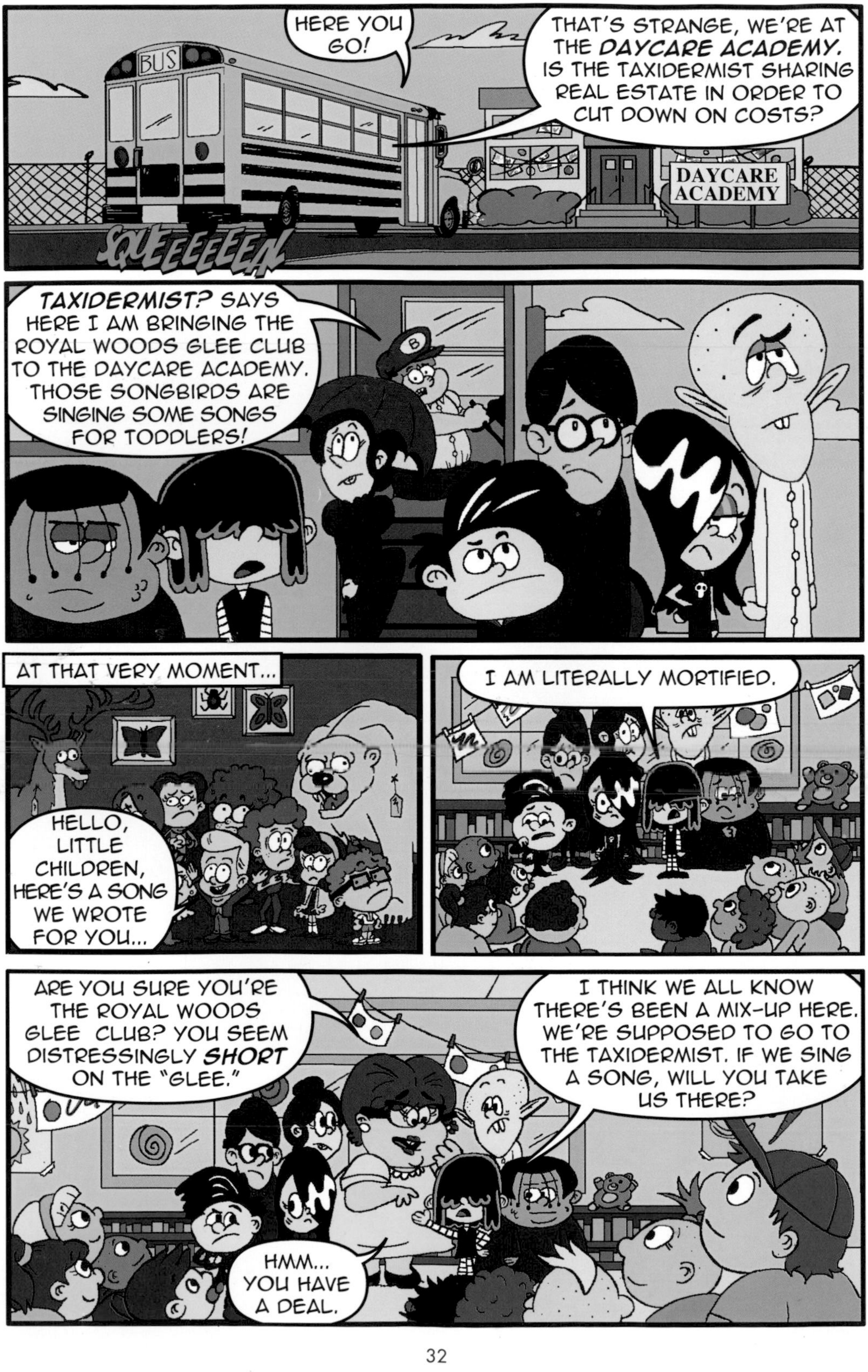
BUS
HERE YOU GO!
THAT'S STRANGE, WE'RE AT THE *DAYCARE ACADEMY.* IS THE TAXIDERMIST SHARING REAL ESTATE IN ORDER TO CUT DOWN ON COSTS?
DAYCARE ACADEMY
SQUEEEEEEEN
TAXIDERMIST? SAYS HERE I AM BRINGING THE ROYAL WOODS GLEE CLUB TO THE DAYCARE ACADEMY. THOSE SONGBIRDS ARE SINGING SOME SONGS FOR TODDLERS!
AT THAT VERY MOMENT...
HELLO, LITTLE CHILDREN, HERE'S A SONG WE WROTE FOR YOU...
I AM LITERALLY MORTIFIED.
ARE YOU SURE YOU'RE THE ROYAL WOODS GLEE CLUB? YOU SEEM DISTRESSINGLY *SHORT* ON THE "GLEE."
I THINK WE ALL KNOW THERE'S BEEN A MIX-UP HERE. WE'RE SUPPOSED TO GO TO THE TAXIDERMIST. IF WE SING A SONG, WILL YOU TAKE US THERE?
HMM... YOU HAVE A DEAL.

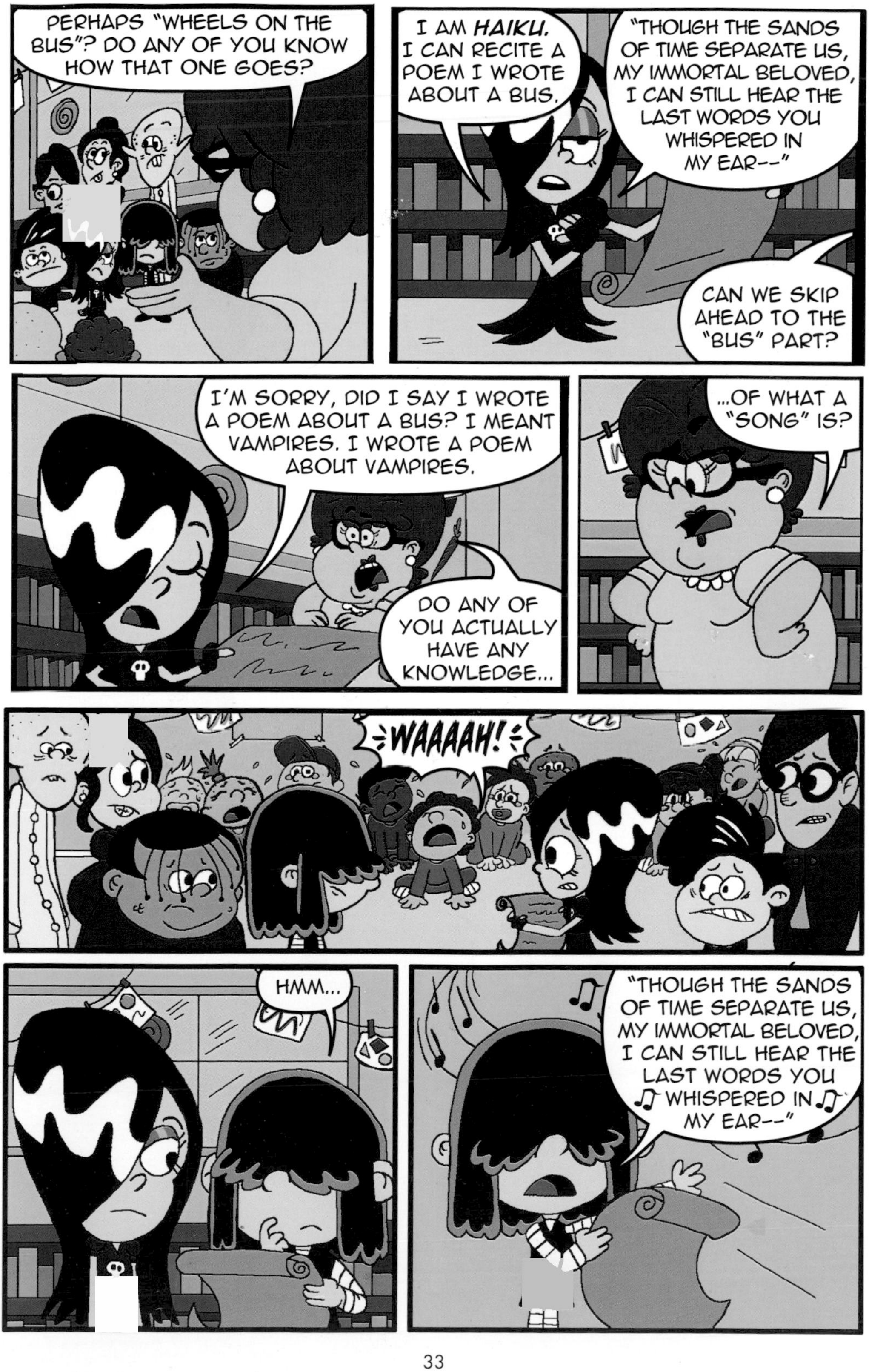
PERHAPS "WHEELS ON THE BUS"? DO ANY OF YOU KNOW HOW THAT ONE GOES?
I AM HAIKU. I CAN RECITE A POEM I WROTE ABOUT A BUS.
"THOUGH THE SANDS OF TIME SEPARATE US, MY IMMORTAL BELOVED, I CAN STILL HEAR THE LAST WORDS YOU WHISPERED IN MY EAR--"
CAN WE SKIP AHEAD TO THE "BUS" PART?
I'M SORRY, DID I SAY I WROTE A POEM ABOUT A BUS? I MEANT VAMPIRES. I WROTE A POEM ABOUT VAMPIRES.
DO ANY OF YOU ACTUALLY HAVE ANY KNOWLEDGE...
...OF WHAT A "SONG" IS?
WAAAAH!
HMM...
"THOUGH THE SANDS OF TIME SEPARATE US, MY IMMORTAL BELOVED, I CAN STILL HEAR THE LAST WORDS YOU WHISPERED IN MY EAR--"

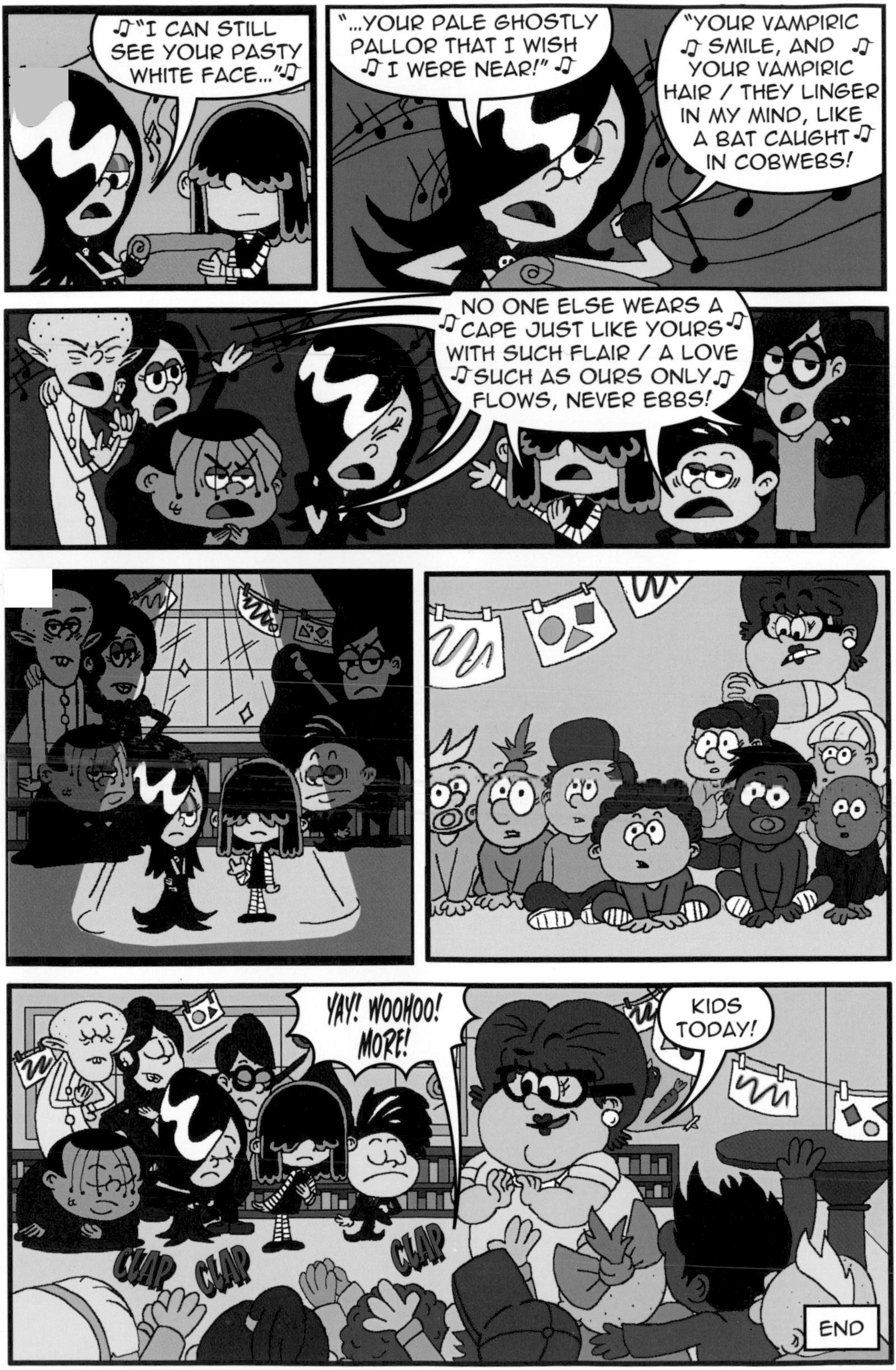
♫"I CAN STILL SEE YOUR PASTY WHITE FACE..."♫
"...YOUR PALE GHOSTLY PALLOR THAT I WISH ♫ I WERE NEAR!" ♫
"YOUR VAMPIRIC ♫ SMILE, AND ♫ YOUR VAMPIRIC HAIR / THEY LINGER IN MY MIND, LIKE A BAT CAUGHT ♫ IN COBWEBS!
NO ONE ELSE WEARS A ♫ CAPE JUST LIKE YOURS ♫ WITH SUCH FLAIR / A LOVE ♫ SUCH AS OURS ONLY ♫ FLOWS, NEVER EBBS!
YAY! WOOHOO! MORE!
KIDS TODAY!
CLAP
CLAP
CLAP
END

"DOWN IN THE DUMPS"

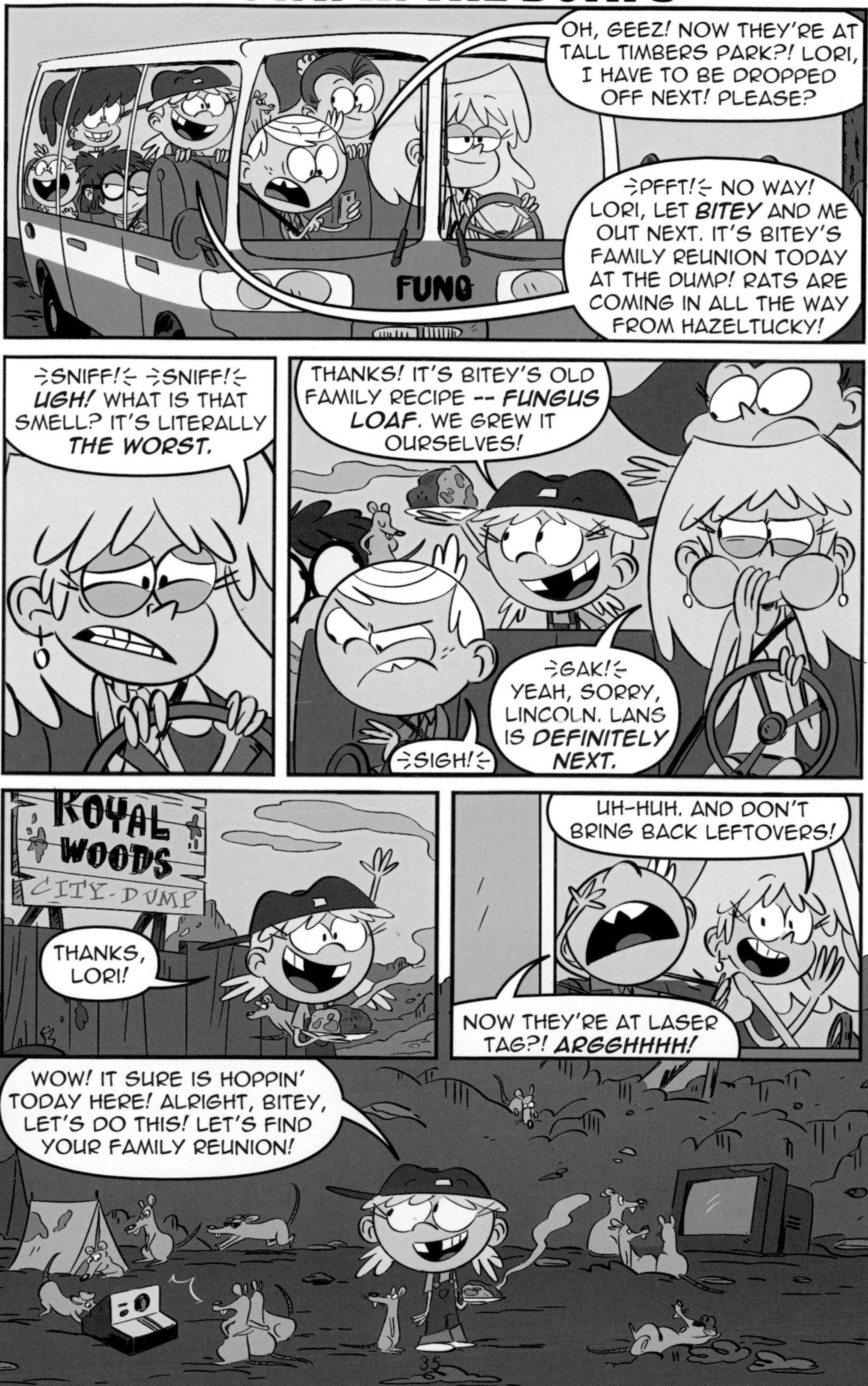
OH, GEEZ! NOW THEY'RE AT TALL TIMBERS PARK?! LORI, I HAVE TO BE DROPPED OFF NEXT! PLEASE?
PFFT! NO WAY! LORI, LET BITEY AND ME OUT NEXT. IT'S BITEY'S FAMILY REUNION TODAY AT THE DUMP! RATS ARE COMING IN ALL THE WAY FROM HAZELTUCKY!
FUNG
SNIFF! SNIFF! UGH! WHAT IS THAT SMELL? IT'S LITERALLY THE WORST.
THANKS! IT'S BITEY'S OLD FAMILY RECIPE -- FUNGUS LOAF. WE GREW IT OURSELVES!
GAK! YEAH, SORRY, LINCOLN. LANS IS DEFINITELY NEXT.
SIGH!
ROYAL WOODS CITY DUMP
THANKS, LORI!
UH-HUH. AND DON'T BRING BACK LEFTOVERS!
NOW THEY'RE AT LASER TAG?! ARGGHHHH!
WOW! IT SURE IS HOPPIN' TODAY HERE! ALRIGHT, BITEY, LET'S DO THIS! LET'S FIND YOUR FAMILY REUNION!

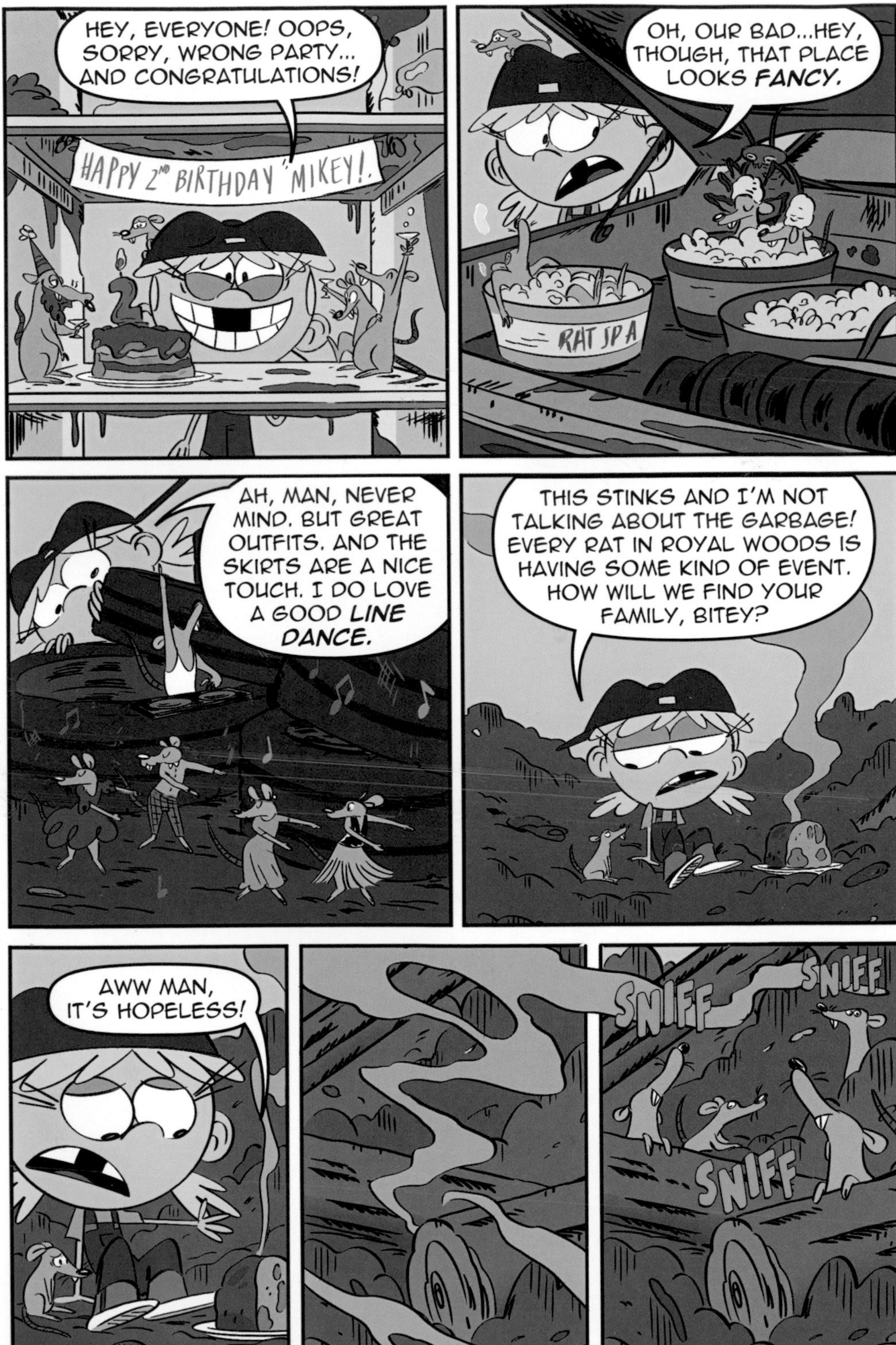
HEY, EVERYONE! OOPS, SORRY, WRONG PARTY... AND CONGRATULATIONS!
HAPPY 2ND BIRTHDAY "MIKEY!"
OH, OUR BAD...HEY, THOUGH, THAT PLACE LOOKS FANCY.
RAT SPA
AH, MAN, NEVER MIND. BUT GREAT OUTFITS. AND THE SKIRTS ARE A NICE TOUCH. I DO LOVE A GOOD LINE DANCE.
THIS STINKS AND I'M NOT TALKING ABOUT THE GARBAGE! EVERY RAT IN ROYAL WOODS IS HAVING SOME KIND OF EVENT. HOW WILL WE FIND YOUR FAMILY, BITEY?
AWW MAN, IT'S HOPELESS!
SNIFF
SNIFF
SNIFF

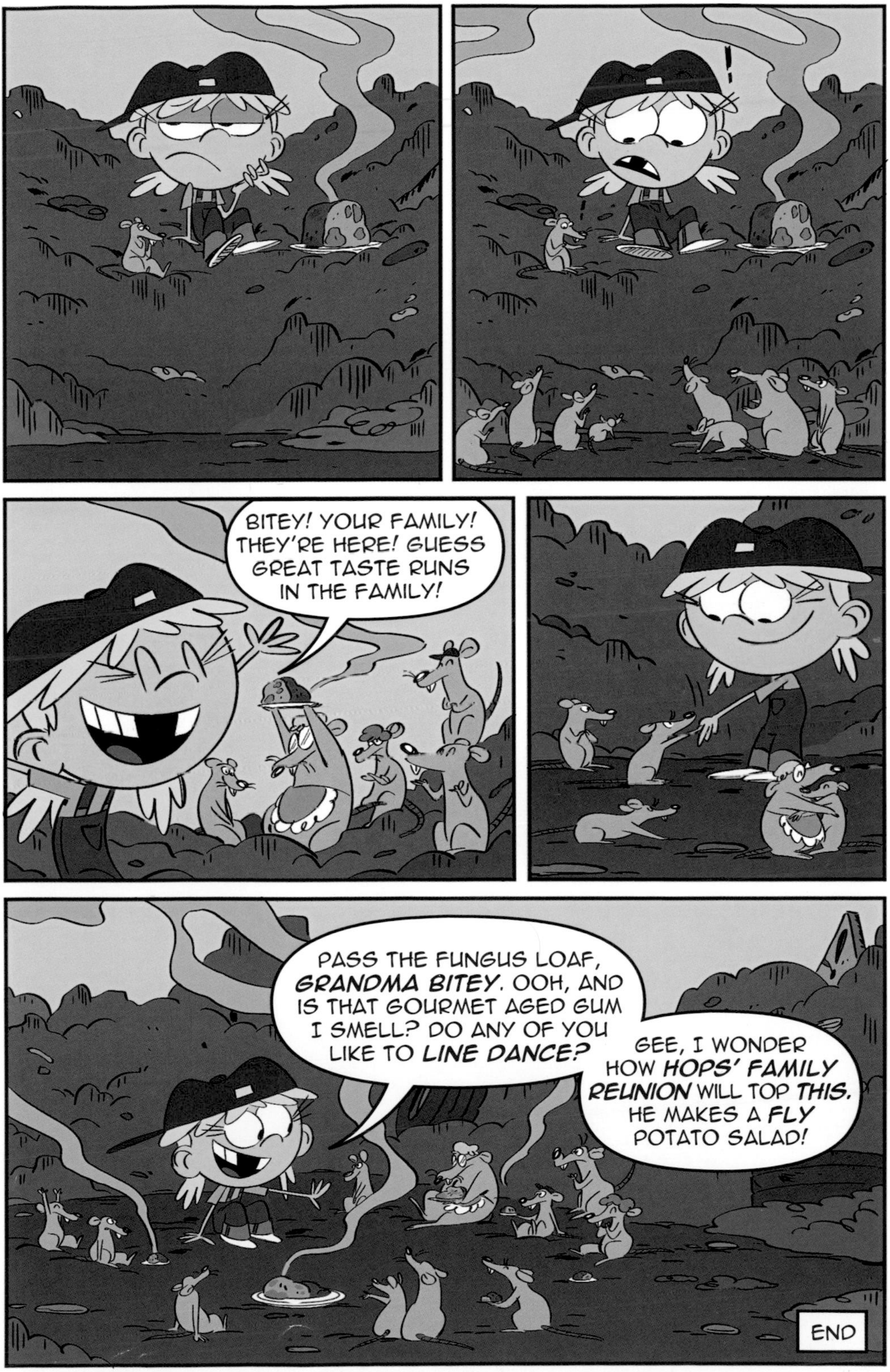
!
BITEY! YOUR FAMILY! THEY'RE HERE! GUESS GREAT TASTE RUNS IN THE FAMILY!
PASS THE FUNGUS LOAF, GRANDMA BITEY. OOH, AND IS THAT GOURMET AGED GUM I SMELL? DO ANY OF YOU LIKE TO LINE DANCE?
GEE, I WONDER HOW HOPS' FAMILY REUNION WILL TOP THIS. HE MAKES A FLY POTATO SALAD!
END

"VAN GO"

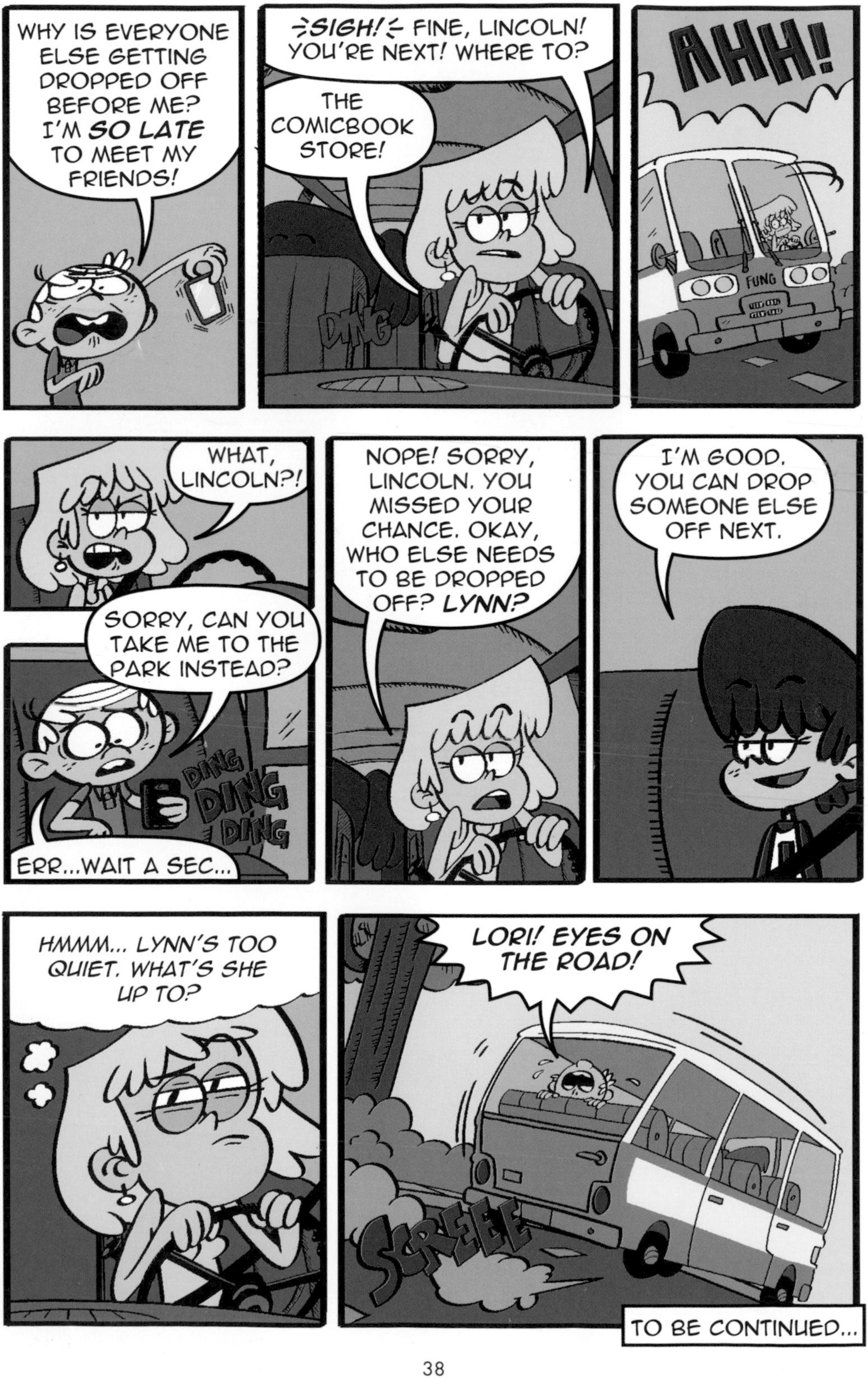
WHY IS EVERYONE ELSE GETTING DROPPED OFF BEFORE ME? I'M SO LATE TO MEET MY FRIENDS!
SIGH! FINE, LINCOLN! YOU'RE NEXT! WHERE TO?
THE COMICBOOK STORE!
DING
AHHH!
FUNG
WHAT, LINCOLN?!
SORRY, CAN YOU TAKE ME TO THE PARK INSTEAD?
DING
DING
DING
ERR...WAIT A SEC...
NOPE! SORRY, LINCOLN. YOU MISSED YOUR CHANCE. OKAY, WHO ELSE NEEDS TO BE DROPPED OFF? LYNN?
I'M GOOD. YOU CAN DROP SOMEONE ELSE OFF NEXT.
HMMM... LYNN'S TOO QUIET. WHAT'S SHE UP TO?
LORI! EYES ON THE ROAD!
SCREEE
TO BE CONTINUED...

"THE GOOD OLD DAYS"

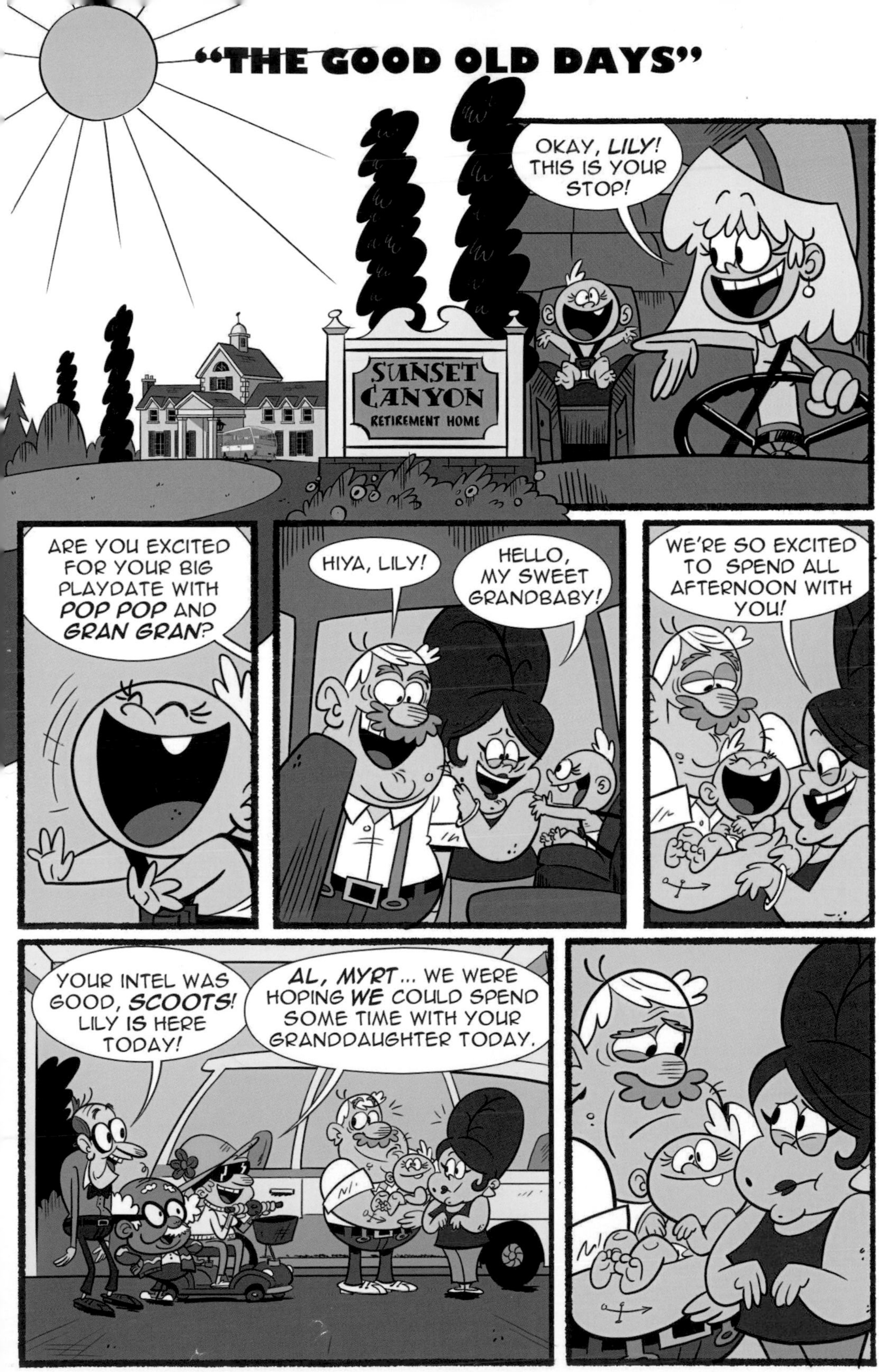
SUNSET CANYON
RETIREMENT HOME
OKAY, LILY! THIS IS YOUR STOP!
ARE YOU EXCITED FOR YOUR BIG PLAYDATE WITH POP POP AND GRAN GRAN?
HIYA, LILY!
HELLO, MY SWEET GRANDBABY!
WE'RE SO EXCITED TO SPEND ALL AFTERNOON WITH YOU!
YOUR INTEL WAS GOOD, SCOOTS! LILY IS HERE TODAY!
AL, MYRT... WE WERE HOPING WE COULD SPEND SOME TIME WITH YOUR GRANDDAUGHTER TODAY.

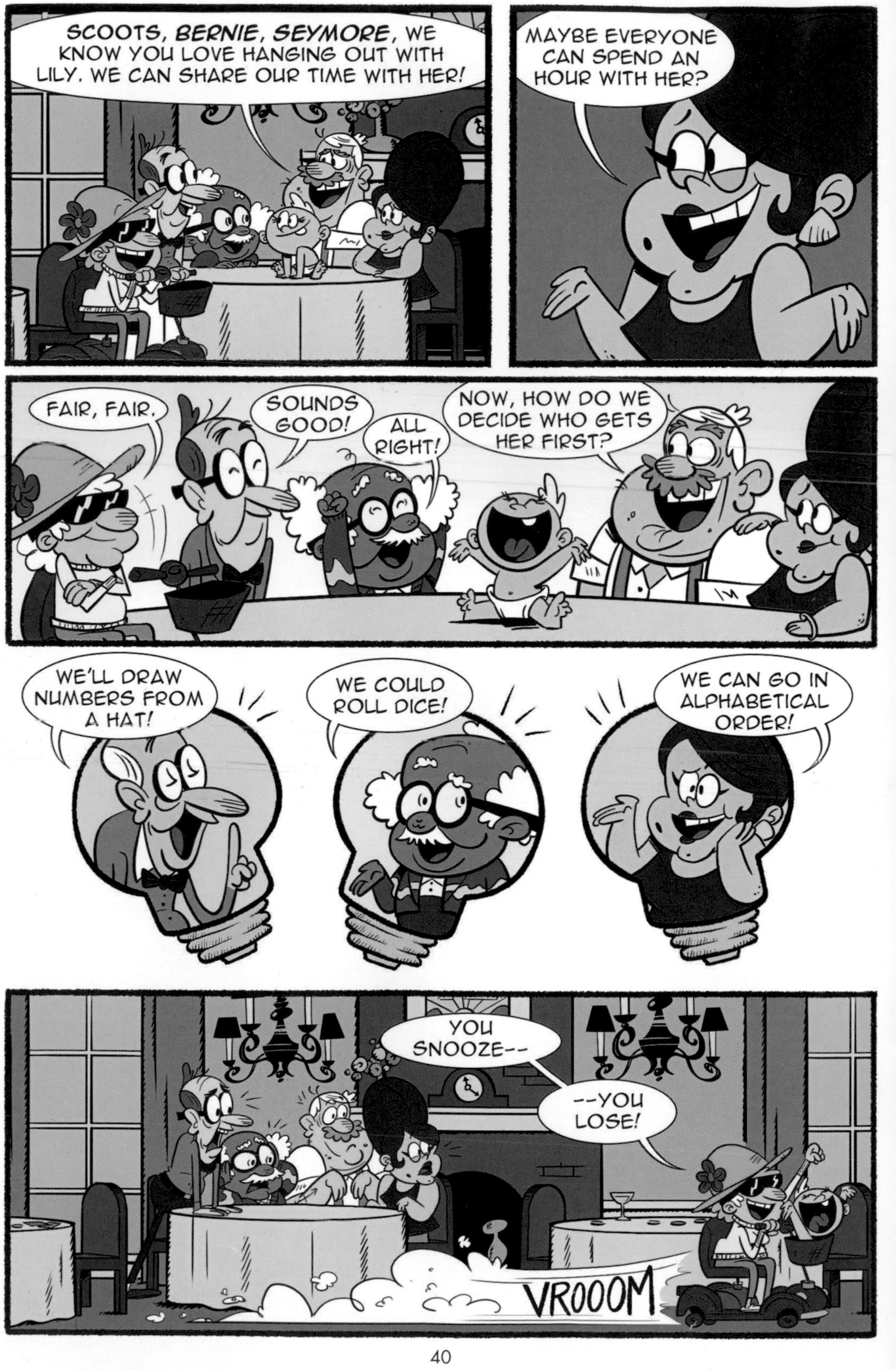
SCOOTS, BERNIE, SEYMORE, WE KNOW YOU LOVE HANGING OUT WITH LILY. WE CAN SHARE OUR TIME WITH HER!
MAYBE EVERYONE CAN SPEND AN HOUR WITH HER?
FAIR, FAIR.
SOUNDS GOOD!
ALL RIGHT!
NOW, HOW DO WE DECIDE WHO GETS HER FIRST?
WE'LL DRAW NUMBERS FROM A HAT!
WE COULD ROLL DICE!
WE CAN GO IN ALPHABETICAL ORDER!
YOU SNOOZE--
--YOU LOSE!
VROOOM

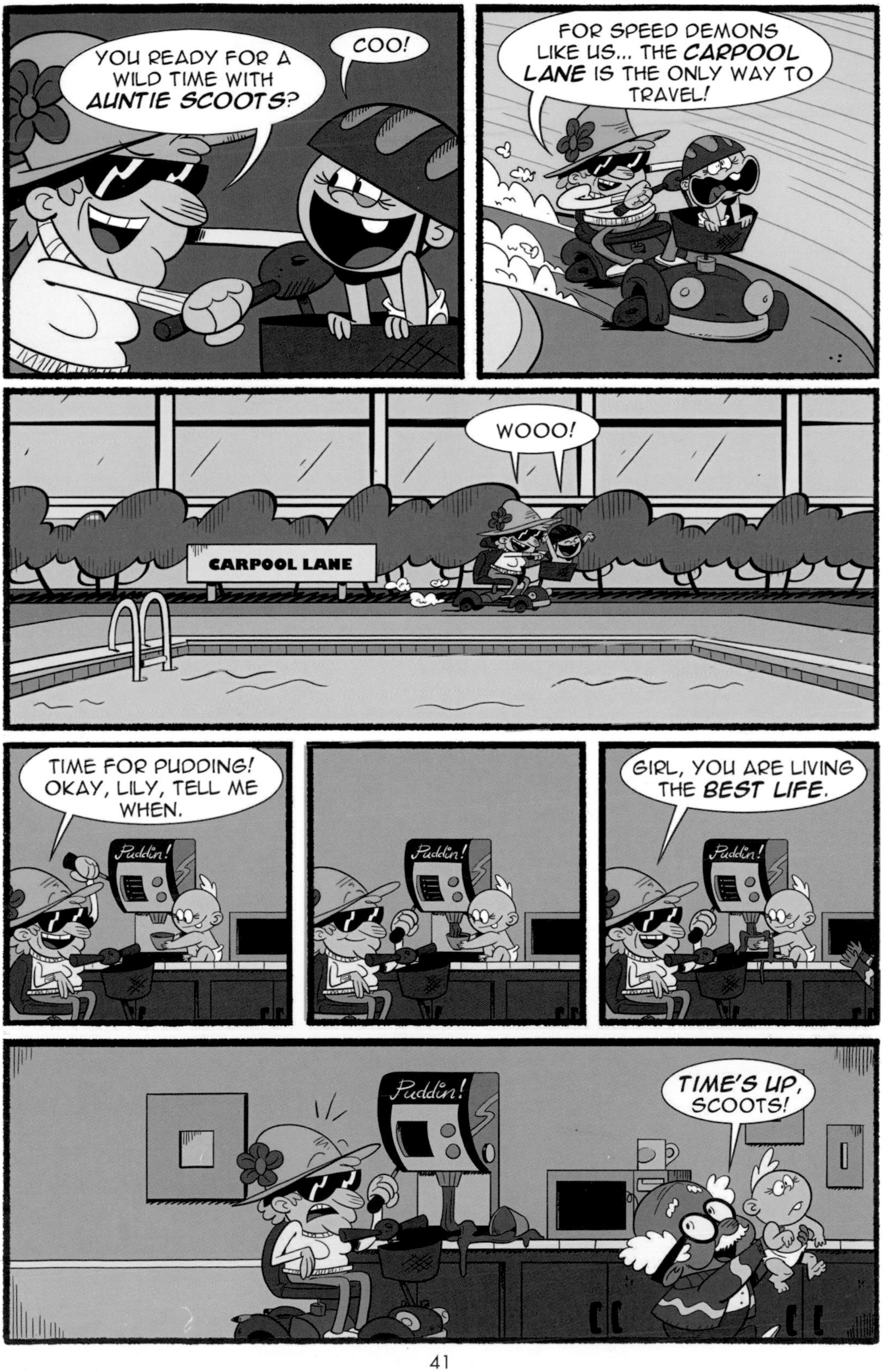
YOU READY FOR A WILD TIME WITH AUNTIE SCOOTS?
COO!
FOR SPEED DEMONS LIKE US... THE CARPOOL LANE IS THE ONLY WAY TO TRAVEL!
WOOO!
CARPOOL LANE
TIME FOR PUDDING! OKAY, LILY, TELL ME WHEN.
Puddin!
Puddin!
GIRL, YOU ARE LIVING THE BEST LIFE.
Puddin!
Puddin!
TIME'S UP, SCOOTS!

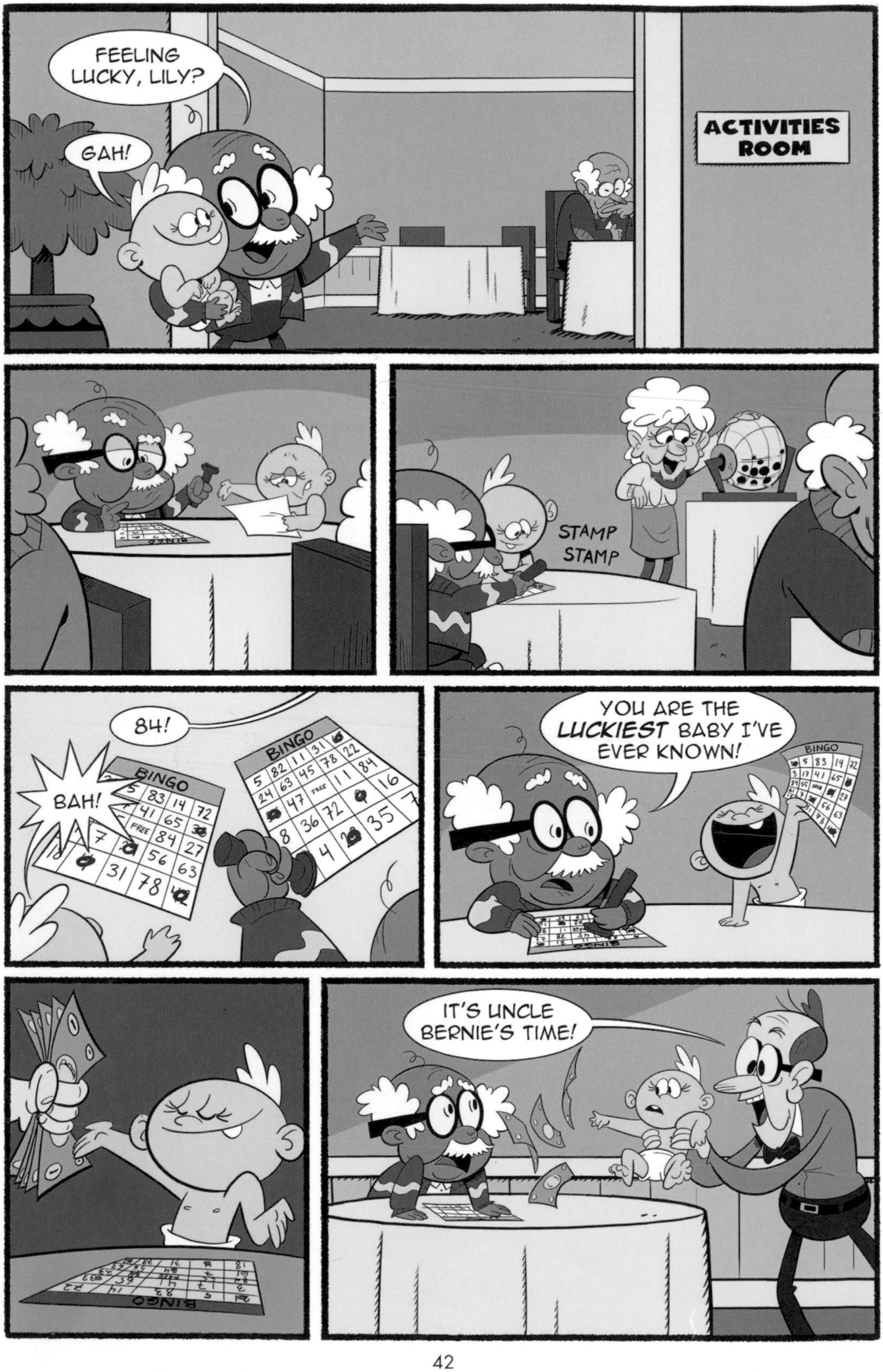
FEELING LUCKY, LILY?
GAH!
ACTIVITIES ROOM
STAMP STAMP
84!
BAH!
YOU ARE THE LUCKIEST BABY I'VE EVER KNOWN!
IT'S UNCLE BERNIE'S TIME!

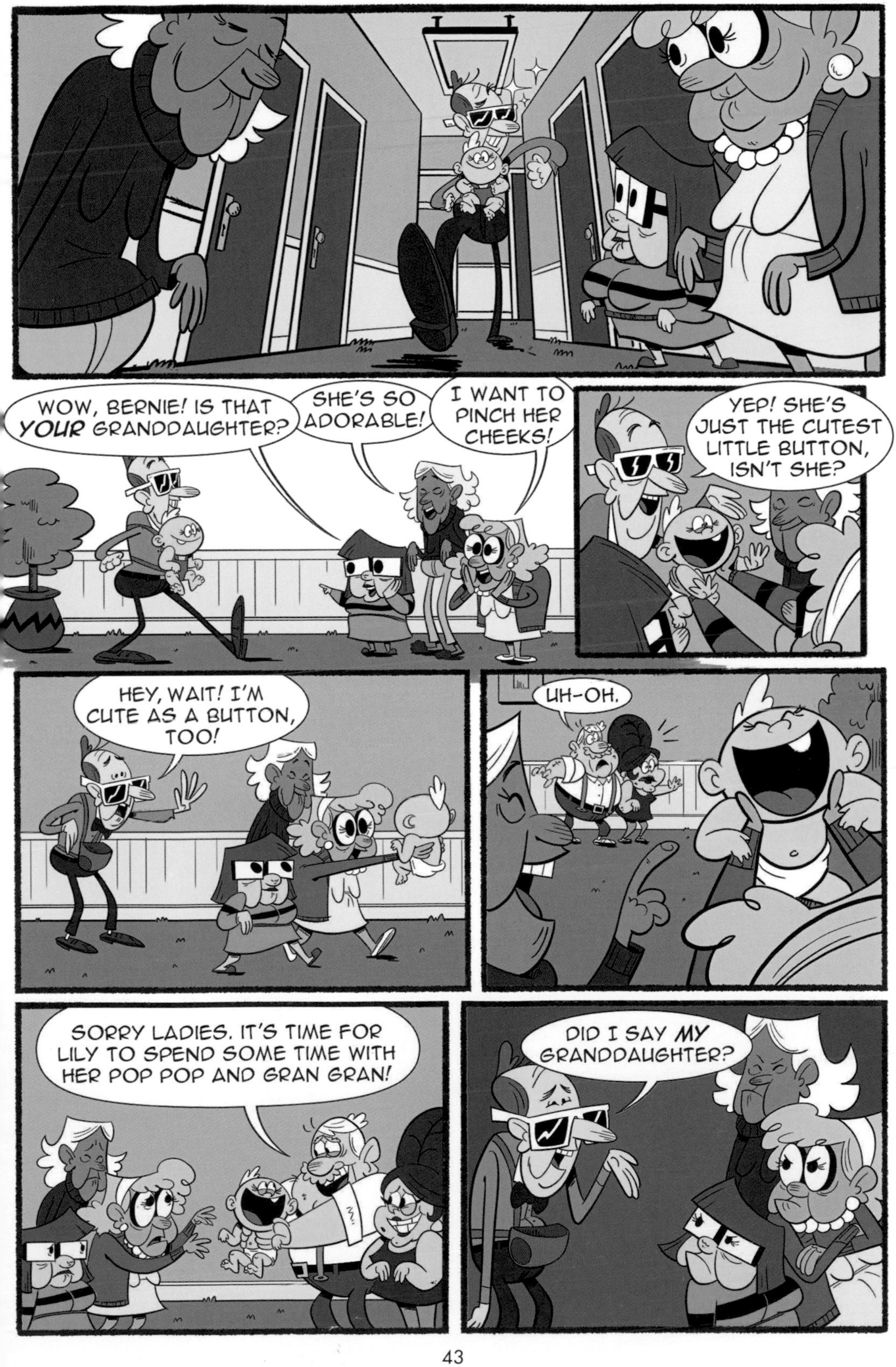
WOW, BERNIE! IS THAT *YOUR* GRANDDAUGHTER?
SHE'S SO ADORABLE!
I WANT TO PINCH HER CHEEKS!
YEP! SHE'S JUST THE CUTEST LITTLE BUTTON, ISN'T SHE?
HEY, WAIT! I'M CUTE AS A BUTTON, TOO!
UH-OH.
SORRY LADIES. IT'S TIME FOR LILY TO SPEND SOME TIME WITH HER POP POP AND GRAN GRAN!
DID I SAY *MY* GRANDDAUGHTER?

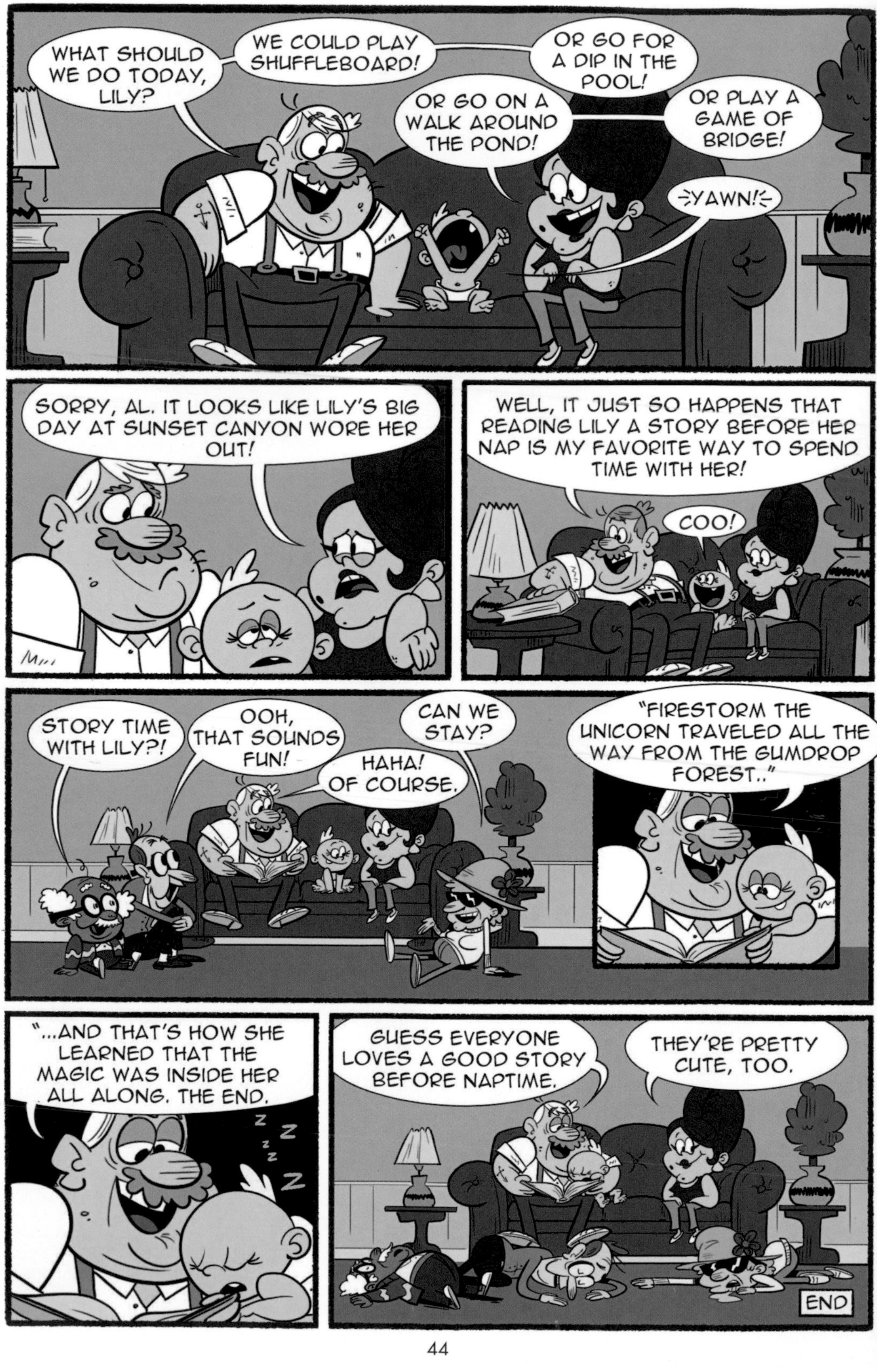
WHAT SHOULD WE DO TODAY, LILY?
WE COULD PLAY SHUFFLEBOARD!
OR GO FOR A DIP IN THE POOL!
OR GO ON A WALK AROUND THE POND!
OR PLAY A GAME OF BRIDGE!
YAWN!
SORRY, AL. IT LOOKS LIKE LILY'S BIG DAY AT SUNSET CANYON WORE HER OUT!
WELL, IT JUST SO HAPPENS THAT READING LILY A STORY BEFORE HER NAP IS MY FAVORITE WAY TO SPEND TIME WITH HER!
COO!
STORY TIME WITH LILY?!
OOH, THAT SOUNDS FUN!
CAN WE STAY?
HAHA! OF COURSE.
"FIRESTORM THE UNICORN TRAVELED ALL THE WAY FROM THE GUMDROP FOREST.."
"...AND THAT'S HOW SHE LEARNED THAT THE MAGIC WAS INSIDE HER ALL ALONG. THE END.
Z Z Z Z Z
GUESS EVERYONE LOVES A GOOD STORY BEFORE NAPTIME.
THEY'RE PRETTY CUTE, TOO.
END

"Hatta Boy"

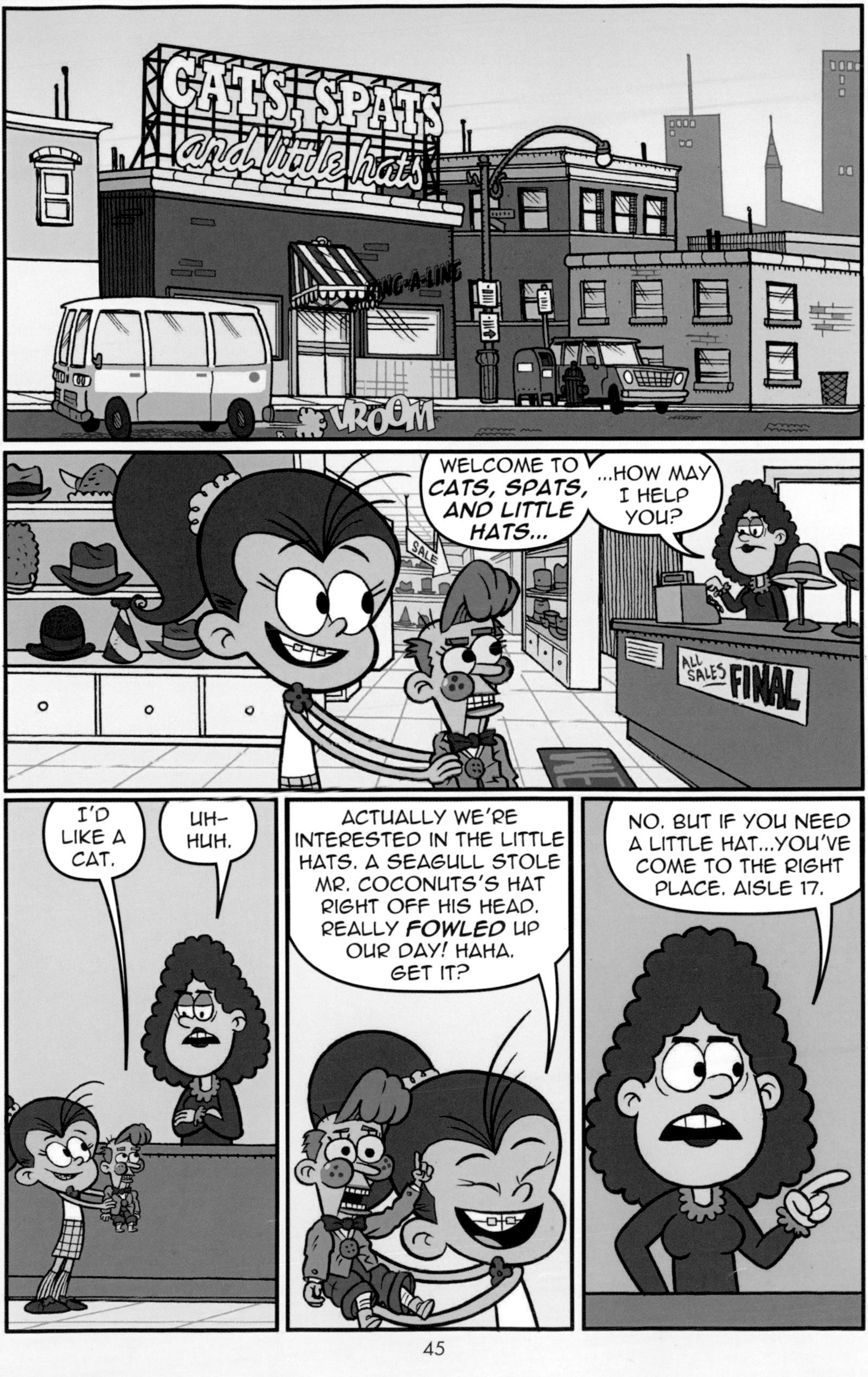
CATS, SPATS and little hats
RING-A-LING
VROOM
SALE
WELCOME TO CATS, SPATS, AND LITTLE HATS...
...HOW MAY I HELP YOU?
ALL SALES FINAL
I'D LIKE A CAT.
UH-HUH.
ACTUALLY WE'RE INTERESTED IN THE LITTLE HATS. A SEAGULL STOLE MR. COCONUTS'S HAT RIGHT OFF HIS HEAD. REALLY *FOWLED* UP OUR DAY! HAHA. GET IT?
NO. BUT IF YOU NEED A LITTLE HAT...YOU'VE COME TO THE RIGHT PLACE. AISLE 17.

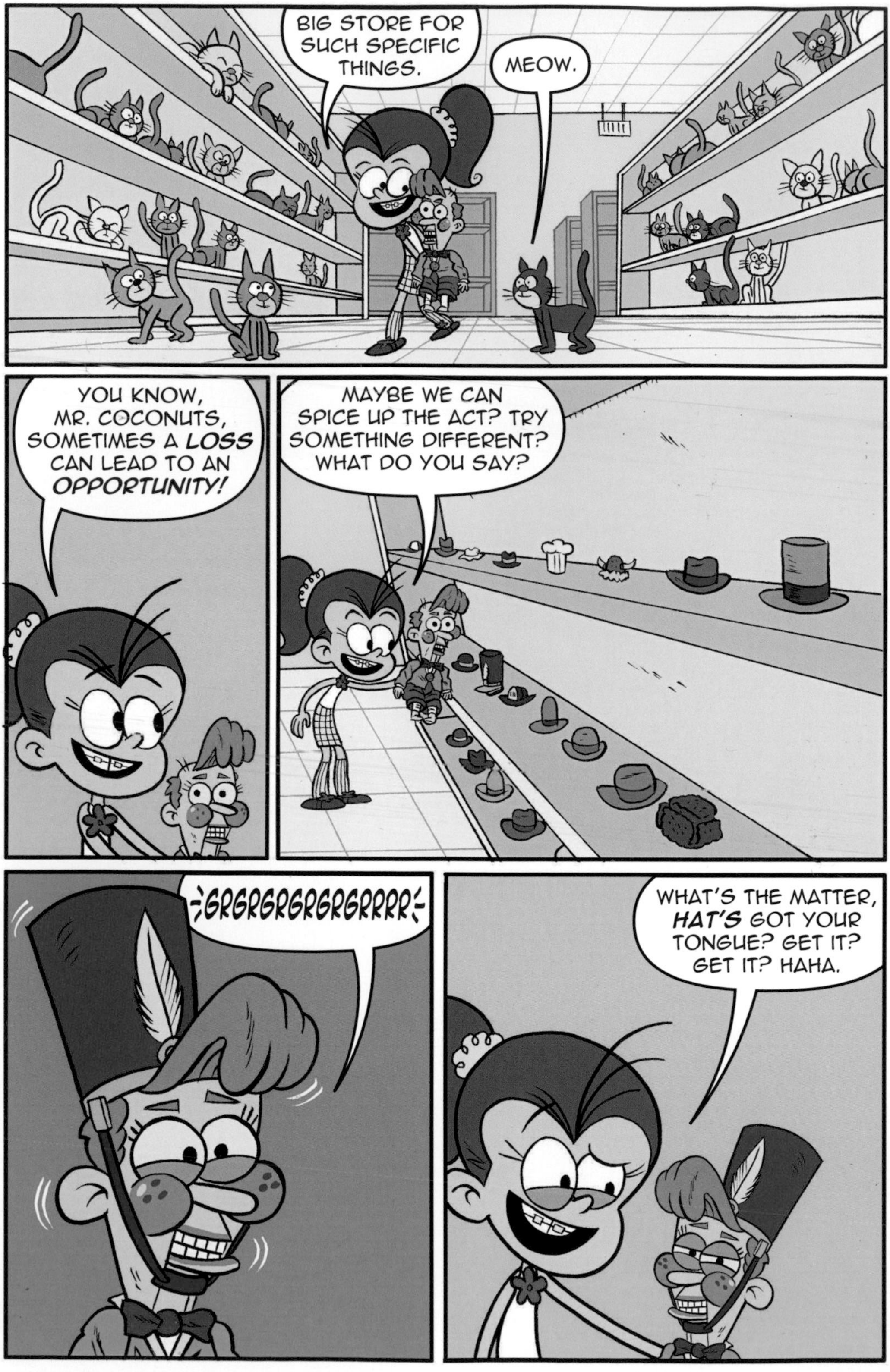
BIG STORE FOR SUCH SPECIFIC THINGS.
MEOW.
YOU KNOW, MR. COCONUTS, SOMETIMES A LOSS CAN LEAD TO AN OPPORTUNITY!
MAYBE WE CAN SPICE UP THE ACT? TRY SOMETHING DIFFERENT? WHAT DO YOU SAY?
GRGRGRGRGRGRRRR
WHAT'S THE MATTER, HAT'S GOT YOUR TONGUE? GET IT? GET IT? HAHA.

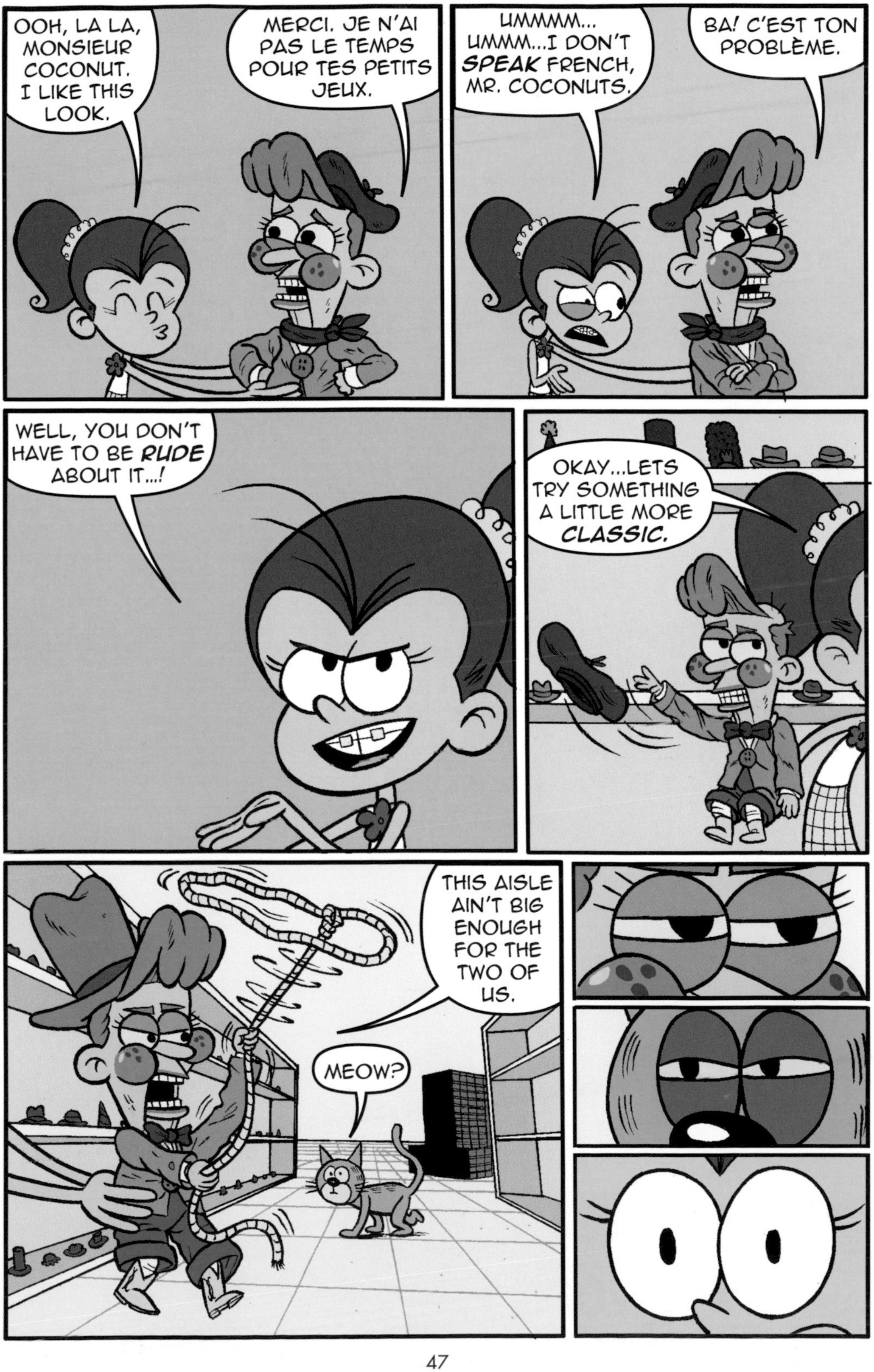
OOH, LA LA, MONSIEUR COCONUT. I LIKE THIS LOOK.
MERCI. JE N'AI PAS LE TEMPS POUR TES PETITS JEUX.
UMMMM... UMMM...I DON'T SPEAK FRENCH, MR. COCONUTS.
BA! C'EST TON PROBLÈME.
WELL, YOU DON'T HAVE TO BE RUDE ABOUT IT...!
OKAY...LETS TRY SOMETHING A LITTLE MORE CLASSIC.
THIS AISLE AIN'T BIG ENOUGH FOR THE TWO OF US.
MEOW?

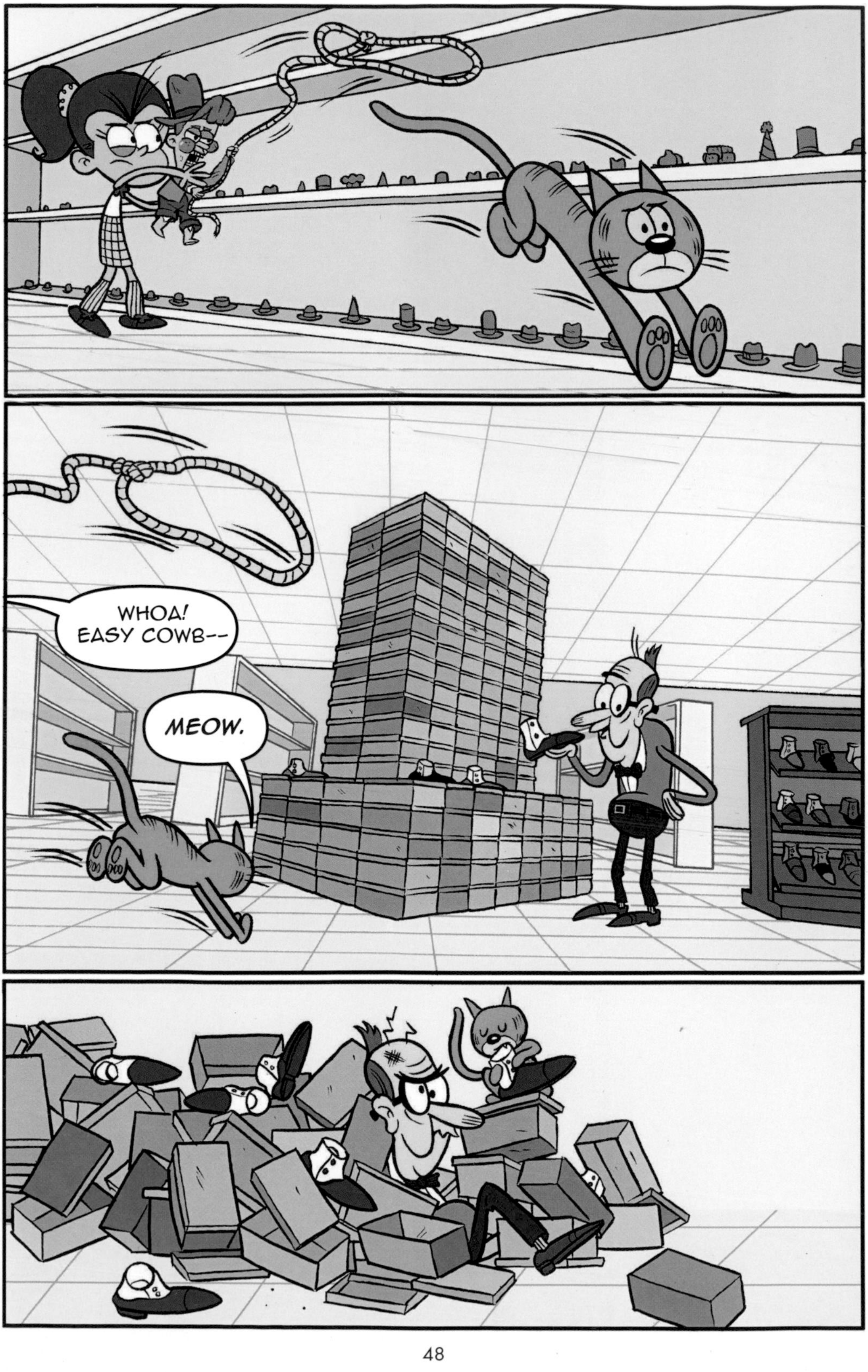
WHOA! EASY COWB--
MEOW.

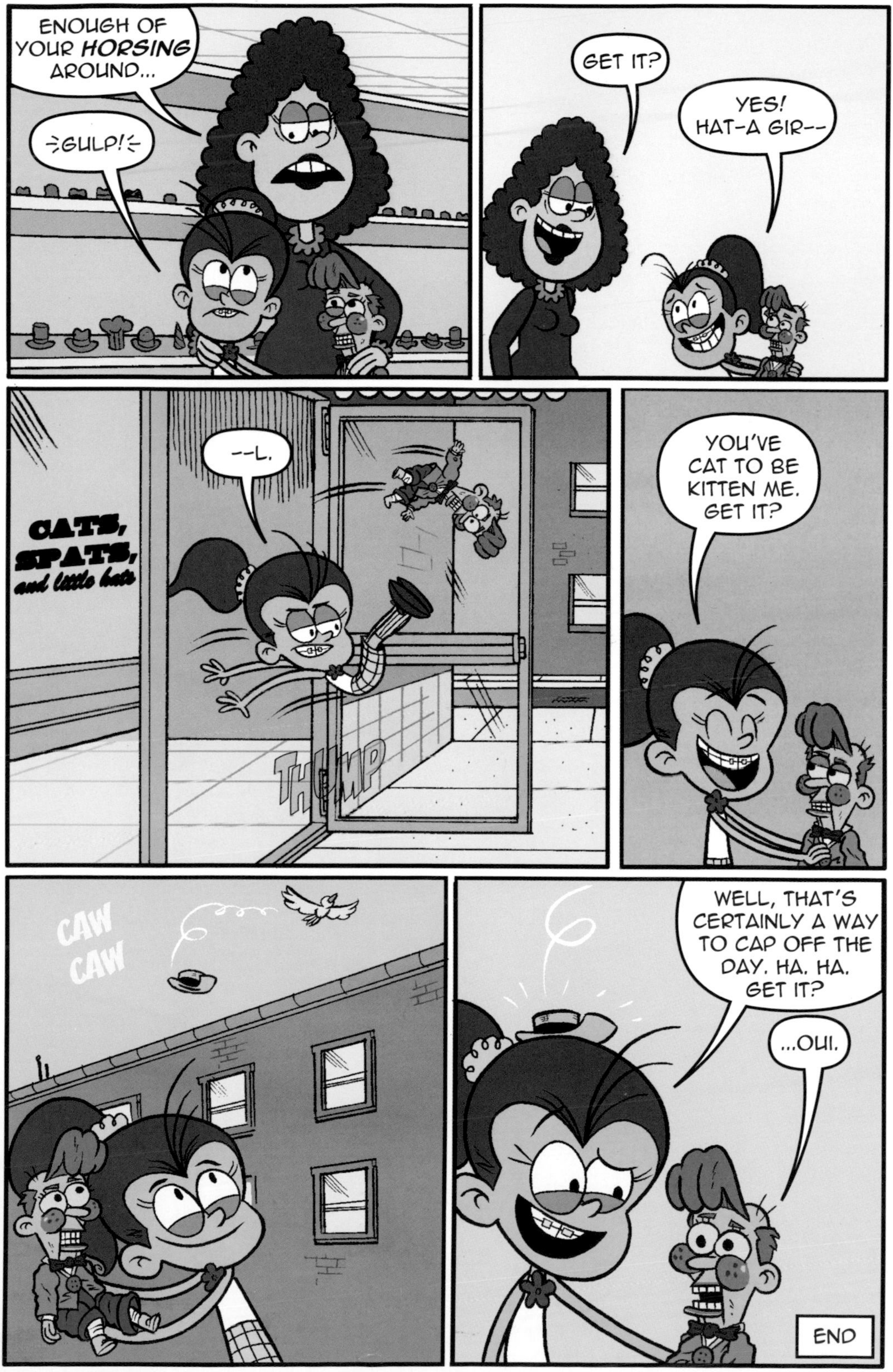
ENOUGH OF YOUR **HORSING** AROUND...
-GULP!-
GET IT?
YES! HAT-A GIR--
--L.
CATS, SPATS, and little hats
THUMP
YOU'VE CAT TO BE KITTEN ME. GET IT?
CAW CAW
WELL, THAT'S CERTAINLY A WAY TO CAP OFF THE DAY. HA. HA. GET IT?
...OUI.
END

"I'M GONNA FINE YOU"

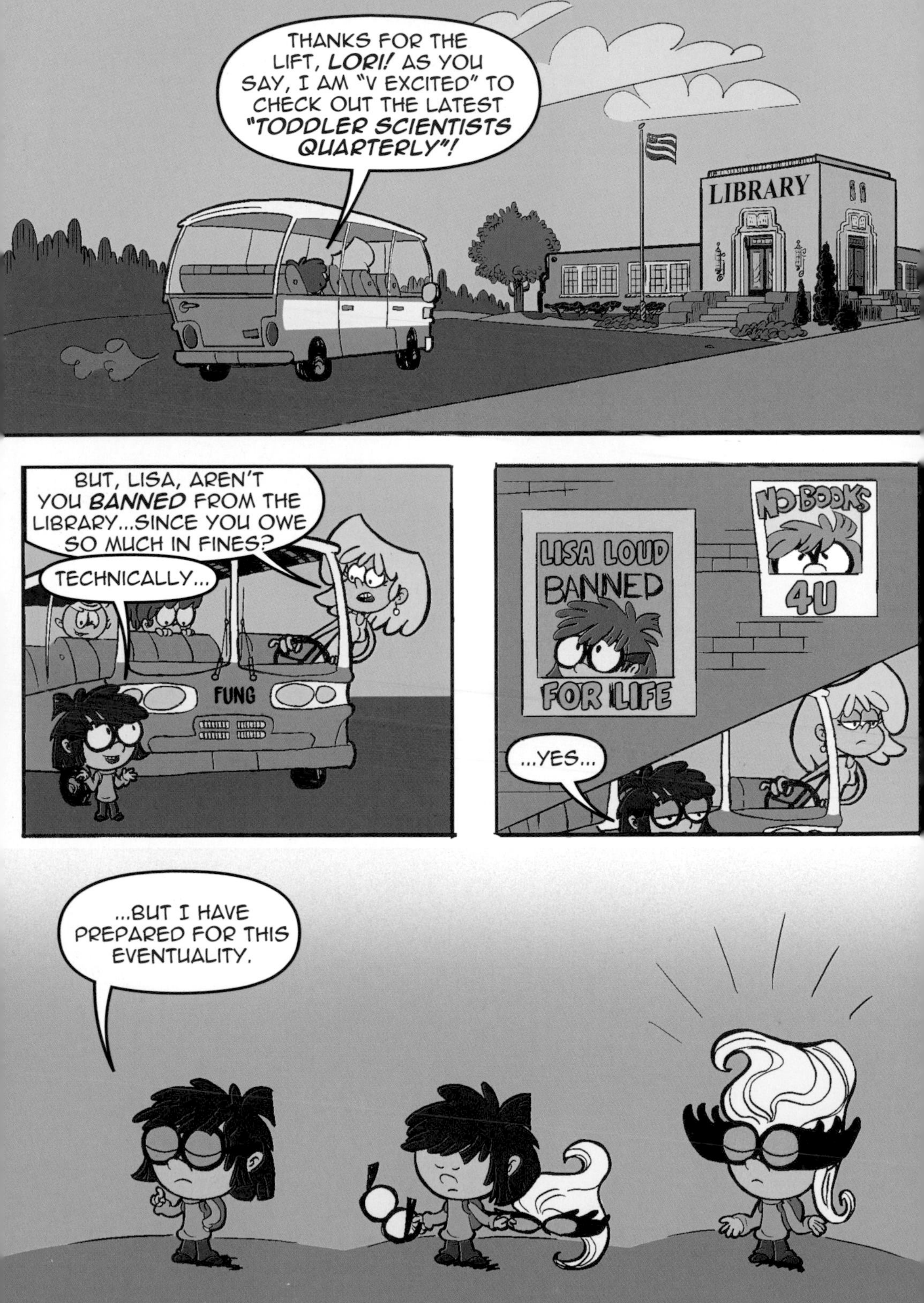
THANKS FOR THE LIFT, LORI! AS YOU SAY, I AM "V EXCITED" TO CHECK OUT THE LATEST "TODDLER SCIENTISTS QUARTERLY"!
LIBRARY
BUT, LISA, AREN'T YOU BANNED FROM THE LIBRARY...SINCE YOU OWE SO MUCH IN FINES?
TECHNICALLY...
FUNG
LISA LOUD BANNED FOR LIFE
NO BOOKS 4U
...YES...
...BUT I HAVE PREPARED FOR THIS EVENTUALITY.

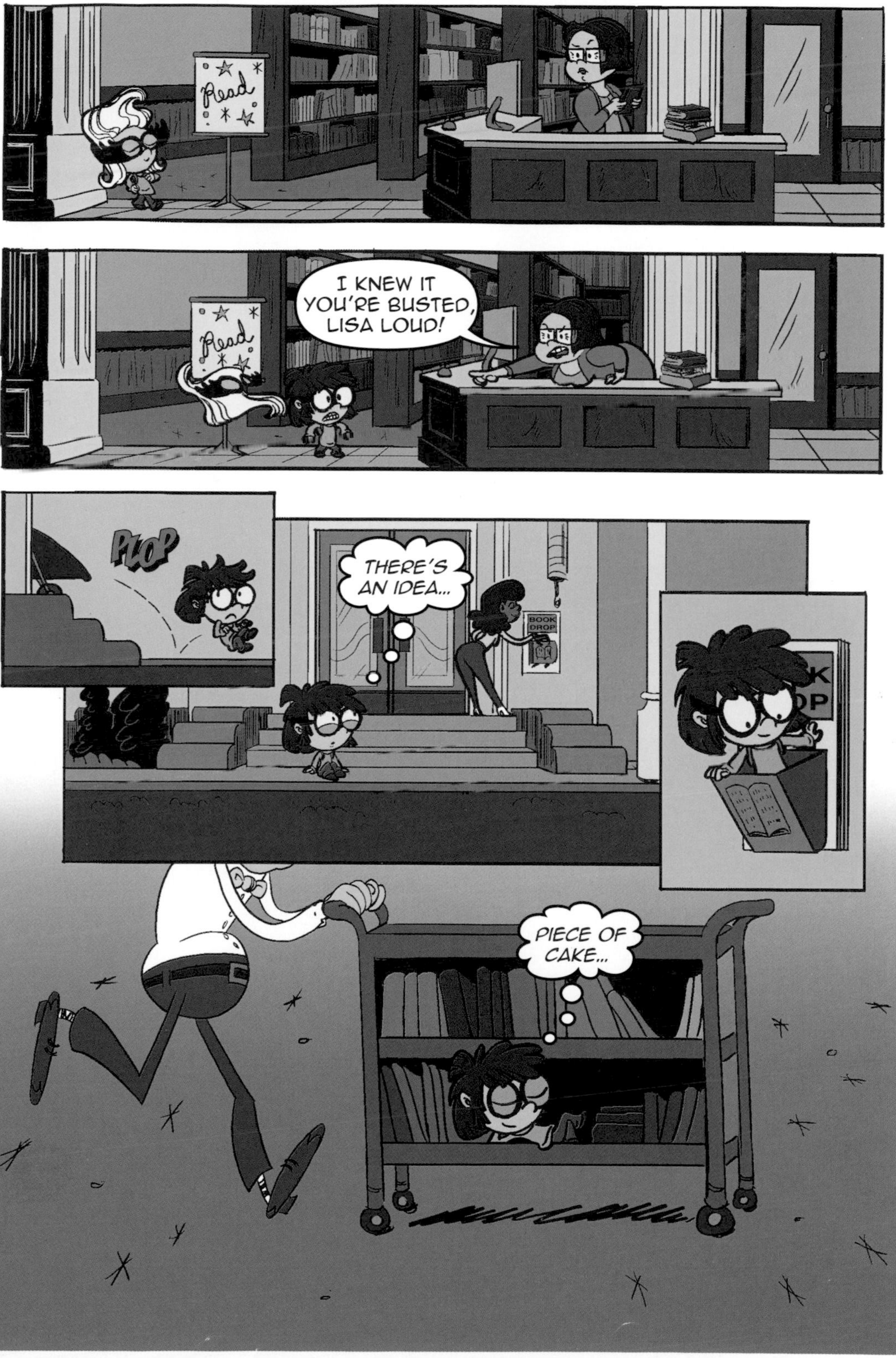

Read
Read
I KNEW IT
YOU'RE BUSTED,
LISA LOUD!
PLOP
THERE'S
AN IDEA...
BOOK
DROP
PIECE OF
CAKE...

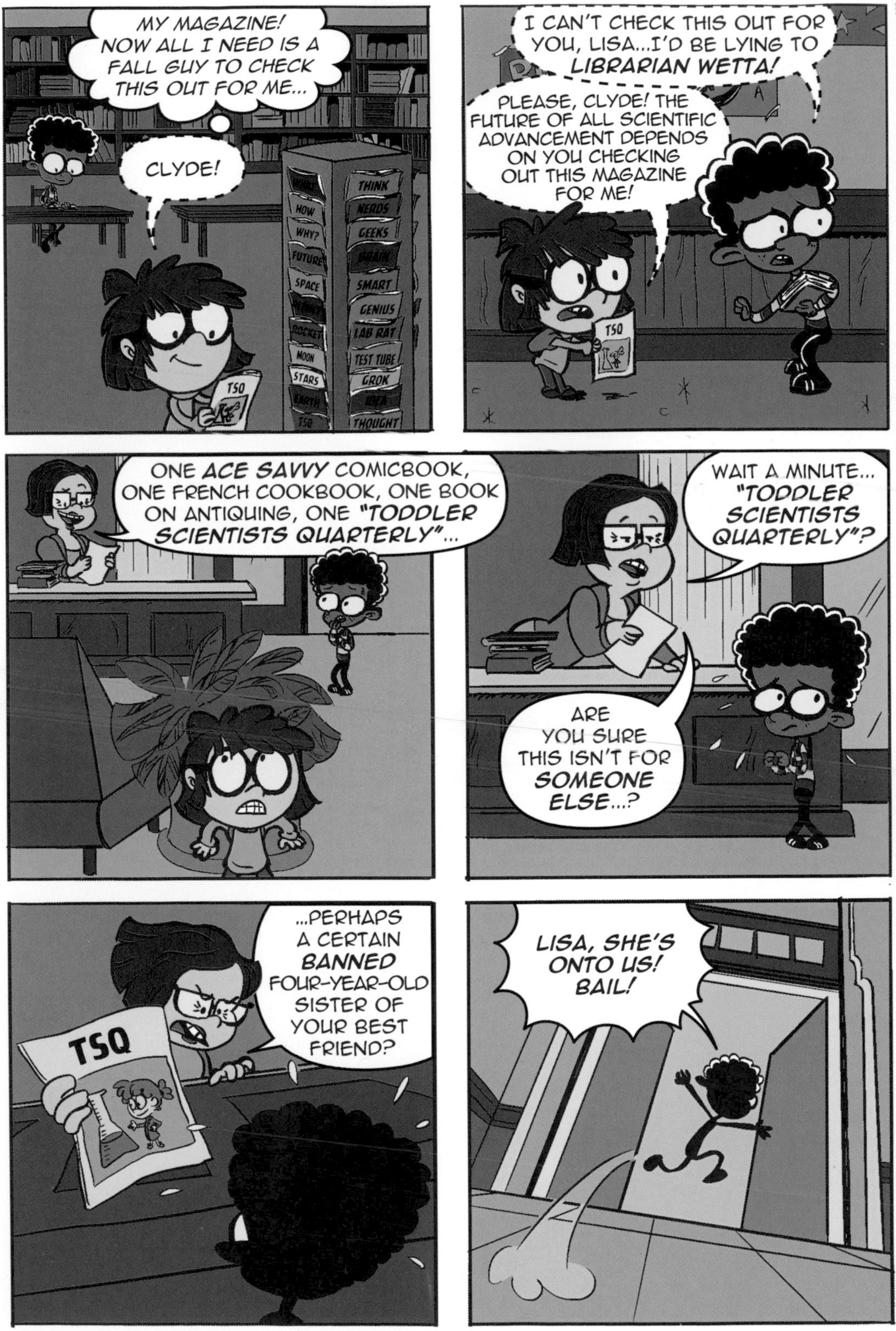
MY MAGAZINE! NOW ALL I NEED IS A FALL GUY TO CHECK THIS OUT FOR ME...
CLYDE!
TSQ
I CAN'T CHECK THIS OUT FOR YOU, LISA...I'D BE LYING TO LIBRARIAN WETTA!
PLEASE, CLYDE! THE FUTURE OF ALL SCIENTIFIC ADVANCEMENT DEPENDS ON YOU CHECKING OUT THIS MAGAZINE FOR ME!
TSQ
ONE ACE SAVVY COMICBOOK, ONE FRENCH COOKBOOK, ONE BOOK ON ANTIQUING, ONE "TODDLER SCIENTISTS QUARTERLY"...
WAIT A MINUTE... "TODDLER SCIENTISTS QUARTERLY"?
ARE YOU SURE THIS ISN'T FOR SOMEONE ELSE...?
...PERHAPS A CERTAIN BANNED FOUR-YEAR-OLD SISTER OF YOUR BEST FRIEND?
TSQ
LISA, SHE'S ONTO US! BAIL!

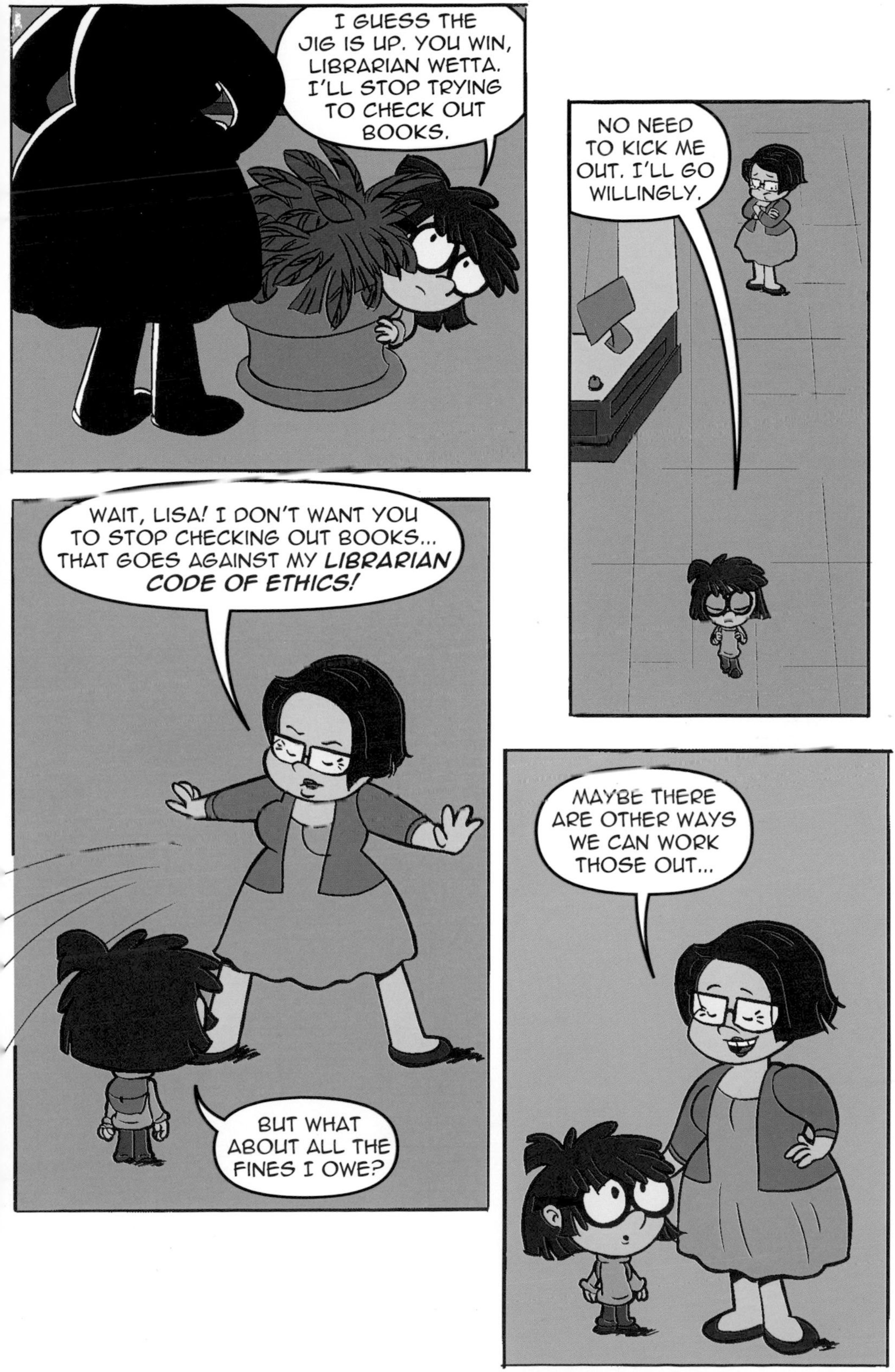
I GUESS THE JIG IS UP. YOU WIN, LIBRARIAN WETTA. I'LL STOP TRYING TO CHECK OUT BOOKS.
NO NEED TO KICK ME OUT. I'LL GO WILLINGLY.
WAIT, LISA! I DON'T WANT YOU TO STOP CHECKING OUT BOOKS... THAT GOES AGAINST MY ***LIBRARIAN CODE OF ETHICS!***
BUT WHAT ABOUT ALL THE FINES I OWE?
MAYBE THERE ARE OTHER WAYS WE CAN WORK THOSE OUT...

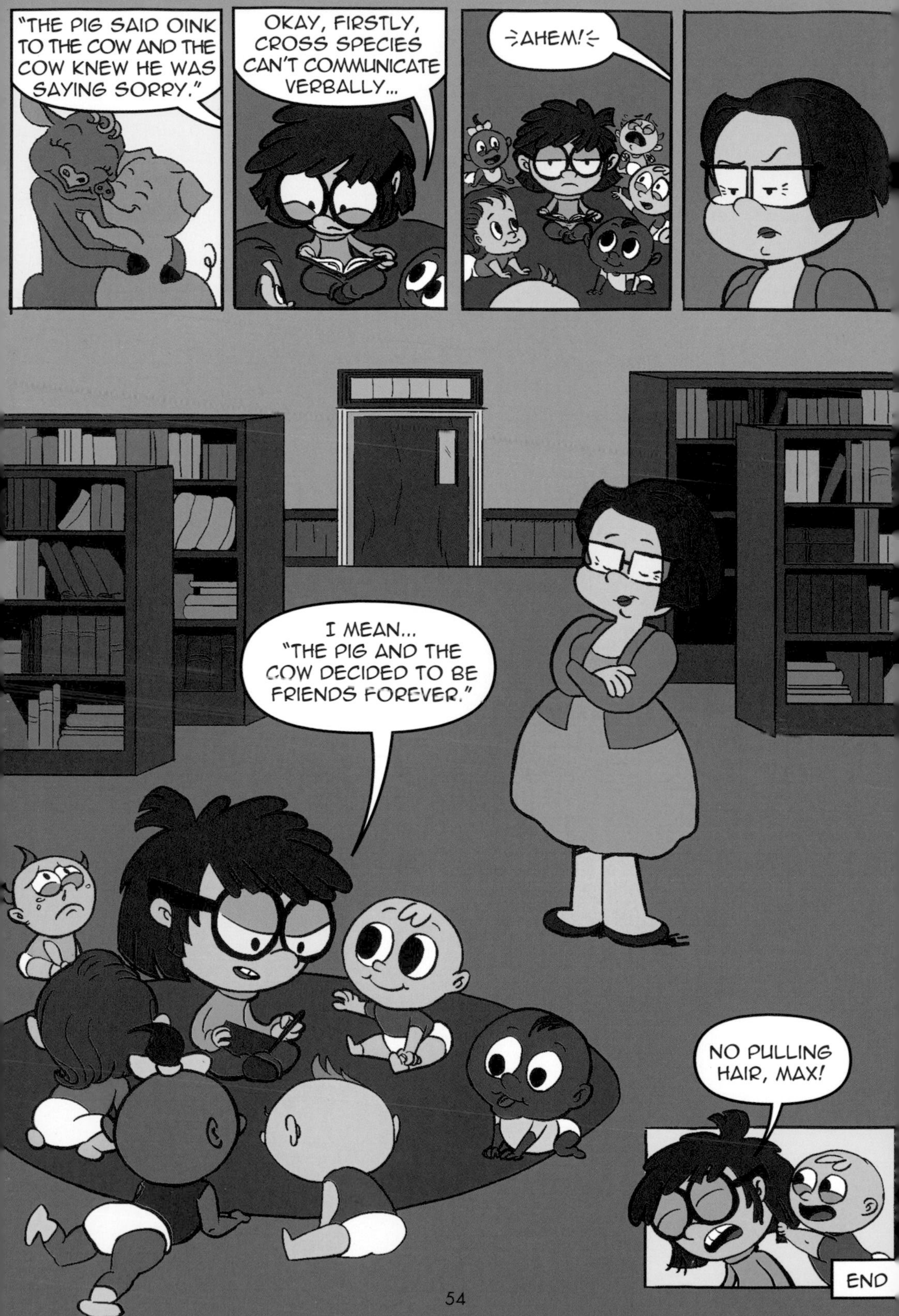
"THE PIG SAID OINK TO THE COW AND THE COW KNEW HE WAS SAYING SORRY."
OKAY, FIRSTLY, CROSS SPECIES CAN'T COMMUNICATE VERBALLY...
AHEM!
I MEAN... "THE PIG AND THE COW DECIDED TO BE FRIENDS FOREVER."
NO PULLING HAIR, MAX!
END

"AN UNEXPECTED JOURNEY"

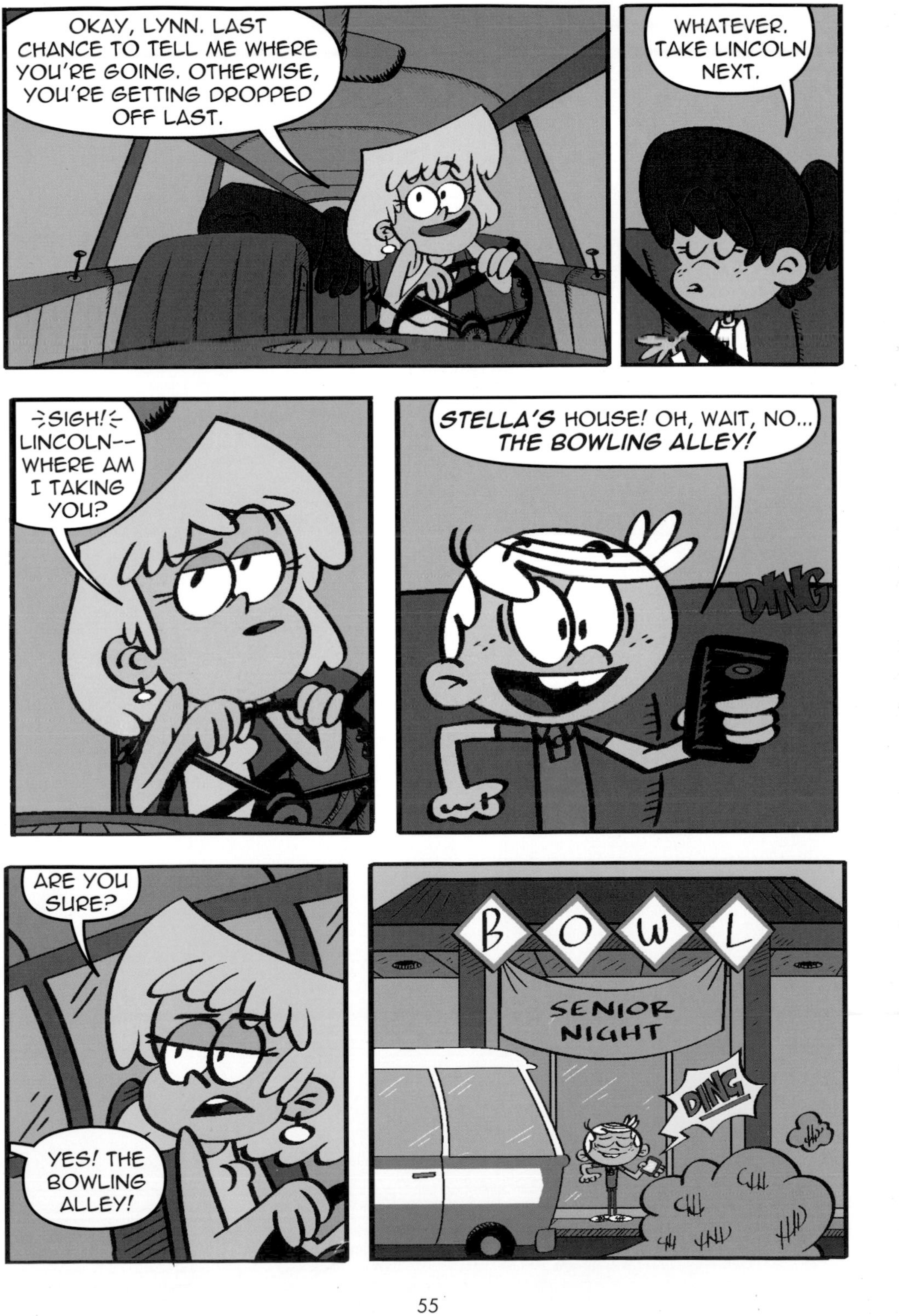
OKAY, LYNN. LAST CHANCE TO TELL ME WHERE YOU'RE GOING. OTHERWISE, YOU'RE GETTING DROPPED OFF LAST.
WHATEVER. TAKE LINCOLN NEXT.
SIGH! LINCOLN-- WHERE AM I TAKING YOU?
STELLA'S HOUSE! OH, WAIT, NO... THE BOWLING ALLEY!
DING
ARE YOU SURE?
YES! THE BOWLING ALLEY!
B O W L
SENIOR NIGHT
DING

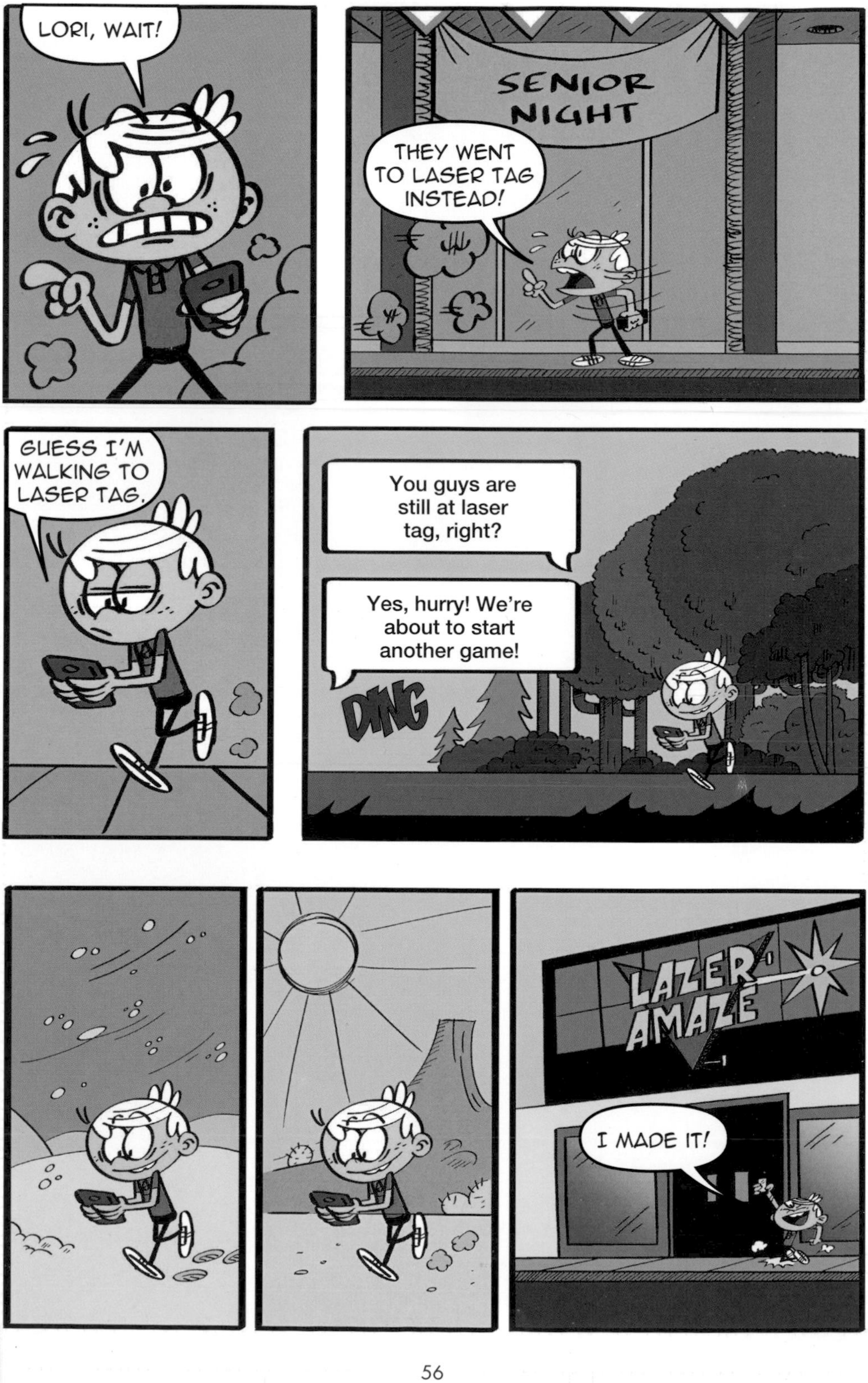
LORI, WAIT!
SENIOR NIGHT
THEY WENT TO LASER TAG INSTEAD!
GUESS I'M WALKING TO LASER TAG.
You guys are still at laser tag, right?
Yes, hurry! We're about to start another game!
DING
LAZER AMAZE
I MADE IT!

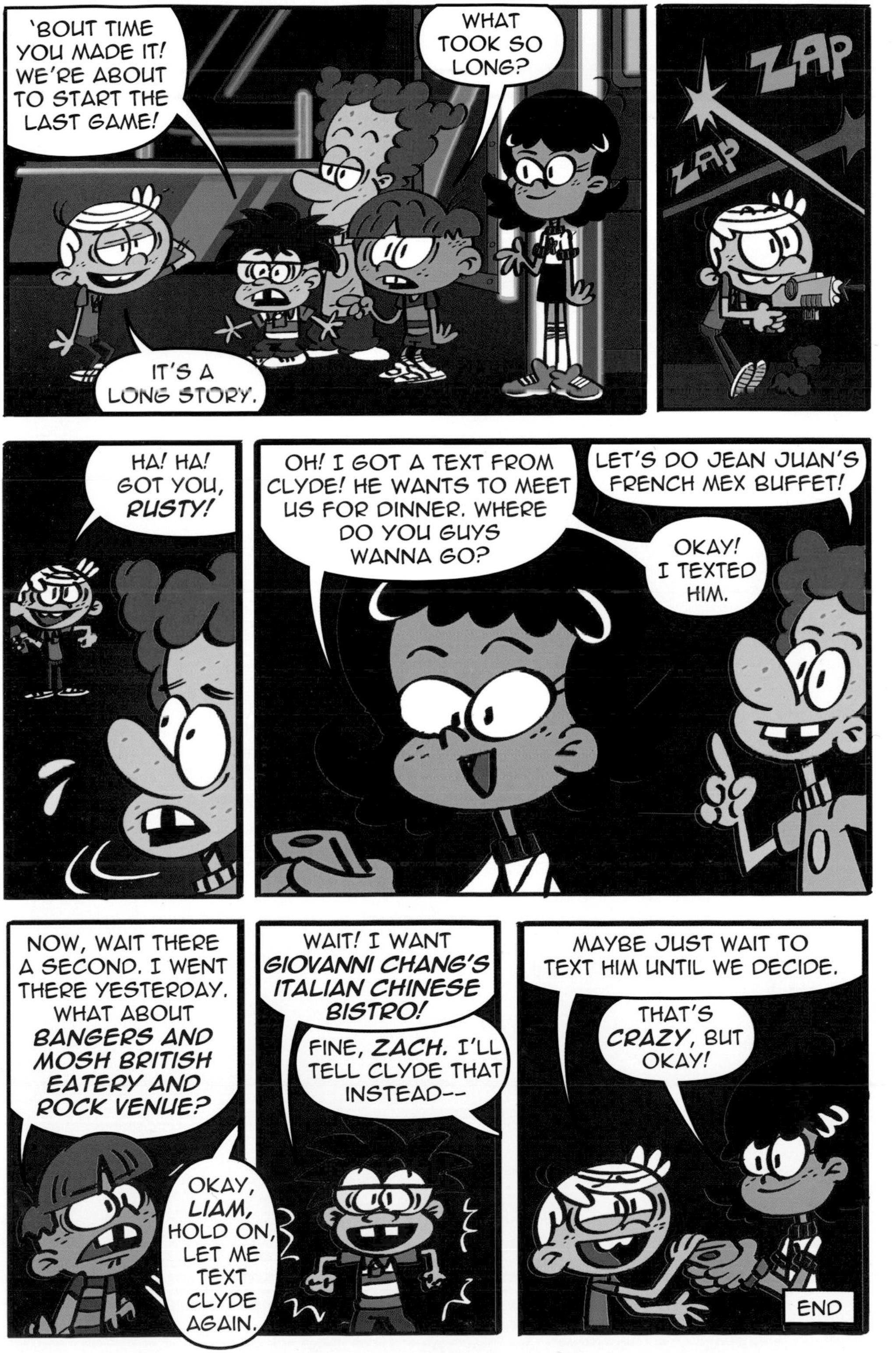

'BOUT TIME YOU MADE IT! WE'RE ABOUT TO START THE LAST GAME!
WHAT TOOK SO LONG?
IT'S A LONG STORY.
ZAP
ZAP
HA! HA! GOT YOU, RUSTY!
OH! I GOT A TEXT FROM CLYDE! HE WANTS TO MEET US FOR DINNER. WHERE DO YOU GUYS WANNA GO?
LET'S DO JEAN JUAN'S FRENCH MEX BUFFET!
OKAY! I TEXTED HIM.
NOW, WAIT THERE A SECOND. I WENT THERE YESTERDAY. WHAT ABOUT BANGERS AND MOSH BRITISH EATERY AND ROCK VENUE?
OKAY, LIAM, HOLD ON, LET ME TEXT CLYDE AGAIN.
WAIT! I WANT GIOVANNI CHANG'S ITALIAN CHINESE BISTRO!
FINE, ZACH. I'LL TELL CLYDE THAT INSTEAD--
MAYBE JUST WAIT TO TEXT HIM UNTIL WE DECIDE.
THAT'S CRAZY, BUT OKAY!
END

"Brag Race"

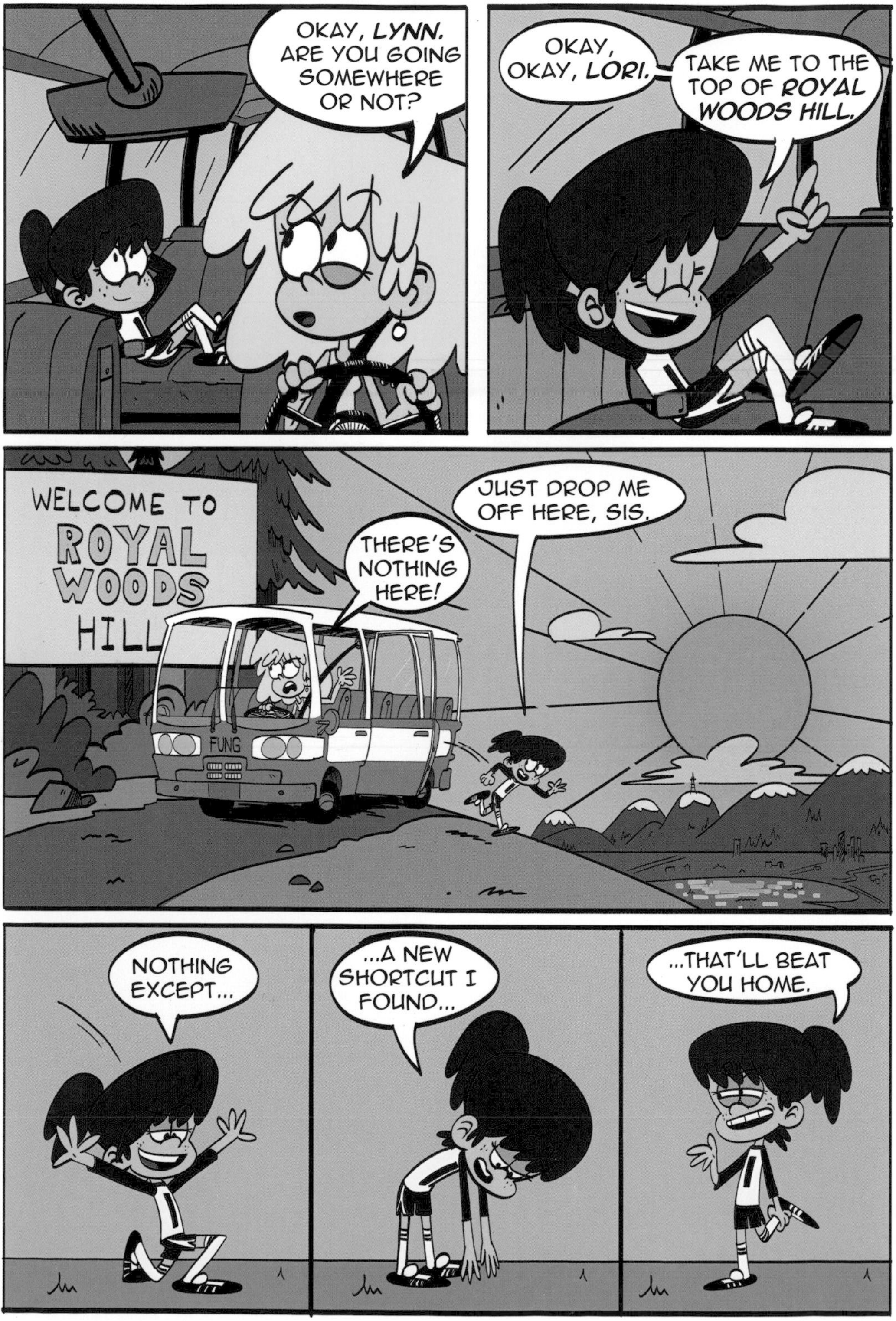

OKAY, LYNN. ARE YOU GOING SOMEWHERE OR NOT?
OKAY, OKAY, LORI.
TAKE ME TO THE TOP OF ROYAL WOODS HILL.
WELCOME TO ROYAL WOODS HILL
JUST DROP ME OFF HERE, SIS.
THERE'S NOTHING HERE!
FUNG
NOTHING EXCEPT...
...A NEW SHORTCUT I FOUND...
...THAT'LL BEAT YOU HOME.

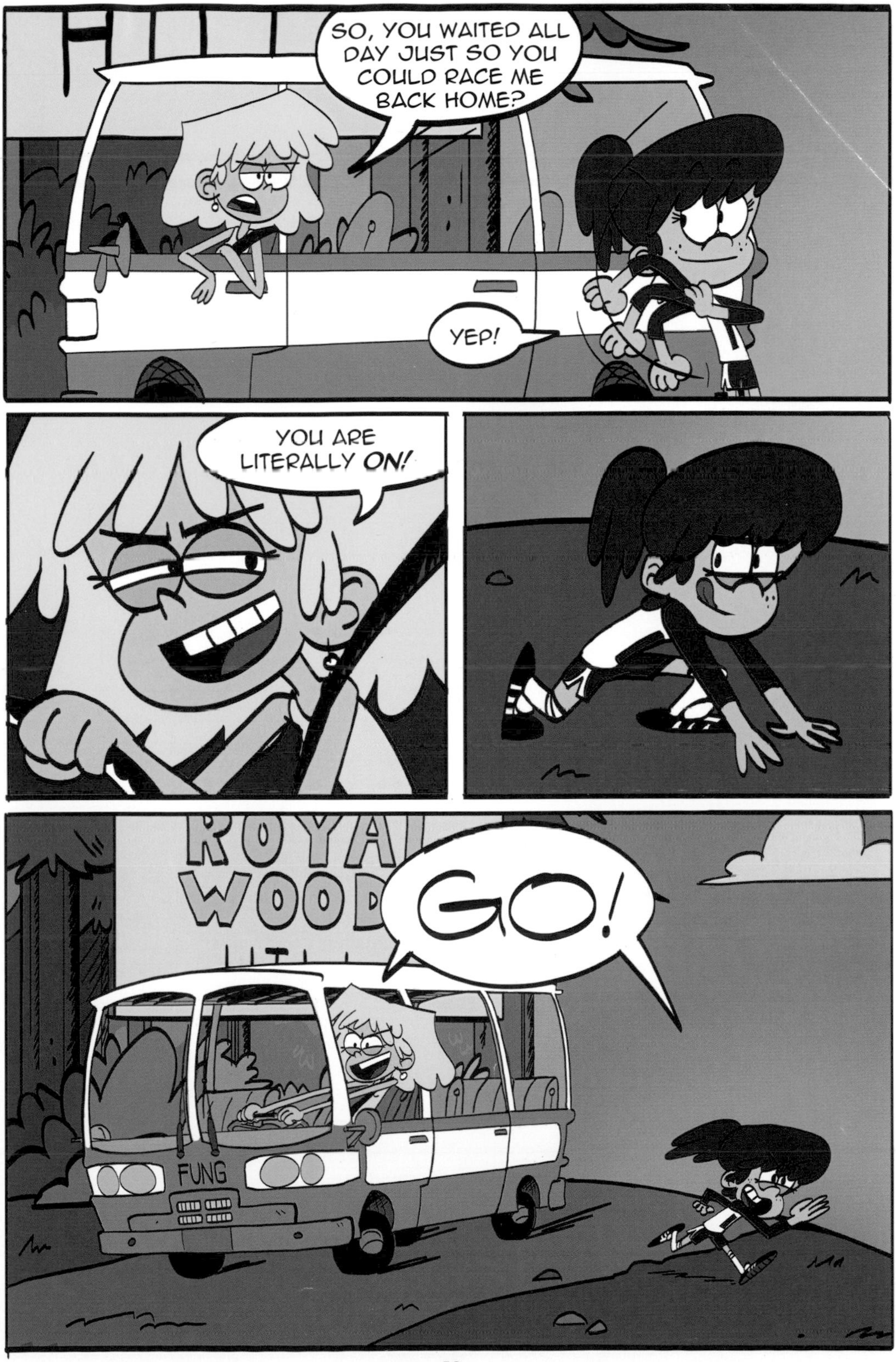
SO, YOU WAITED ALL DAY JUST SO YOU COULD RACE ME BACK HOME?
YEP!
YOU ARE LITERALLY ON!
ROYAL WOOD
GO!
FUNG

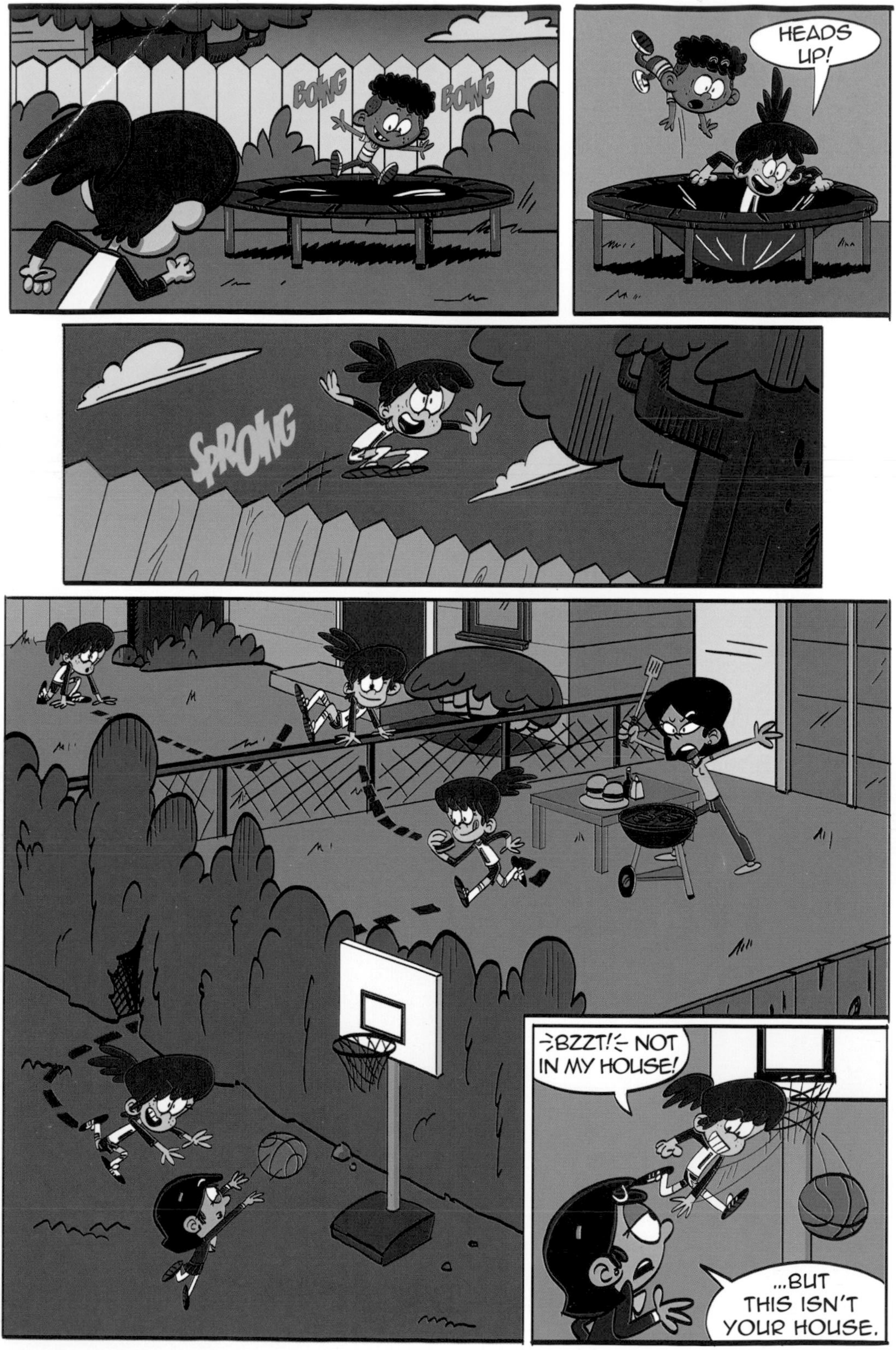
BOING
BOING
HEADS UP!
SPROING
BZZT! NOT IN MY HOUSE!
...BUT THIS ISN'T YOUR HOUSE.

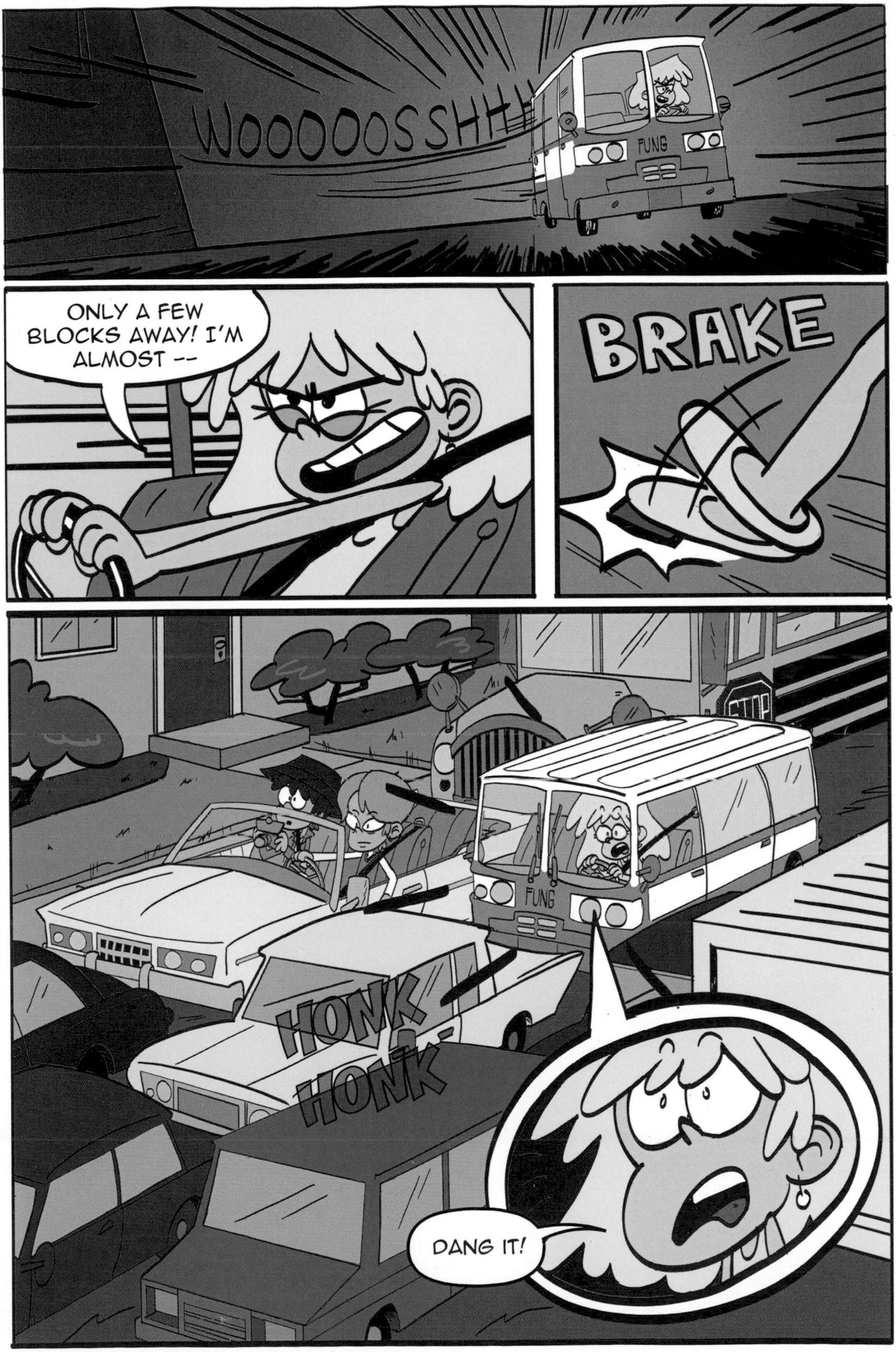
WOOOOOSSHH
FUNG
ONLY A FEW BLOCKS AWAY! I'M ALMOST --
BRAKE
STOP
FUNG
HONK
HONK
DANG IT!

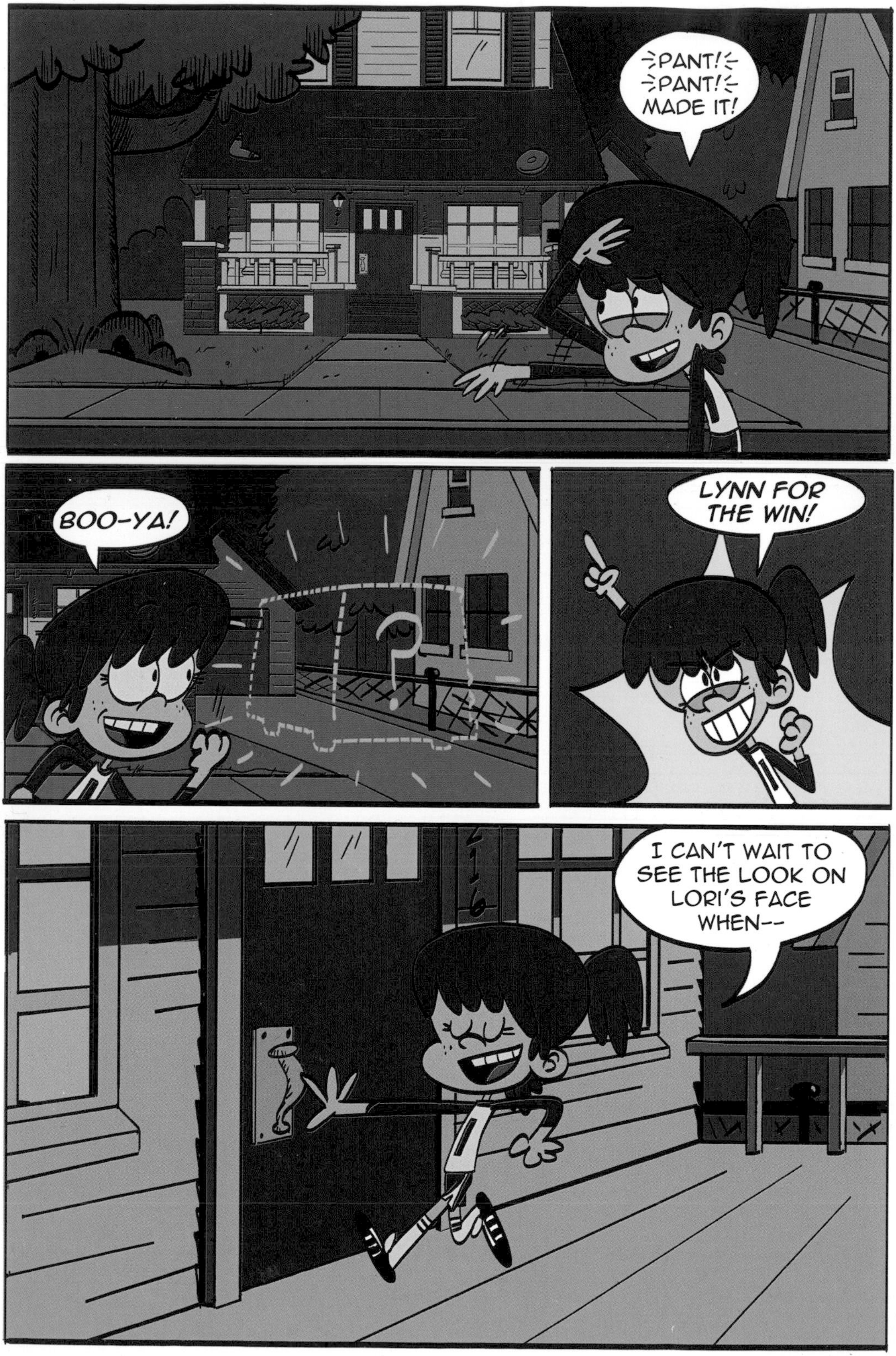
PANT! PANT! MADE IT!
BOO-YA!
LYNN FOR THE WIN!
I CAN'T WAIT TO SEE THE LOOK ON LORI'S FACE WHEN--

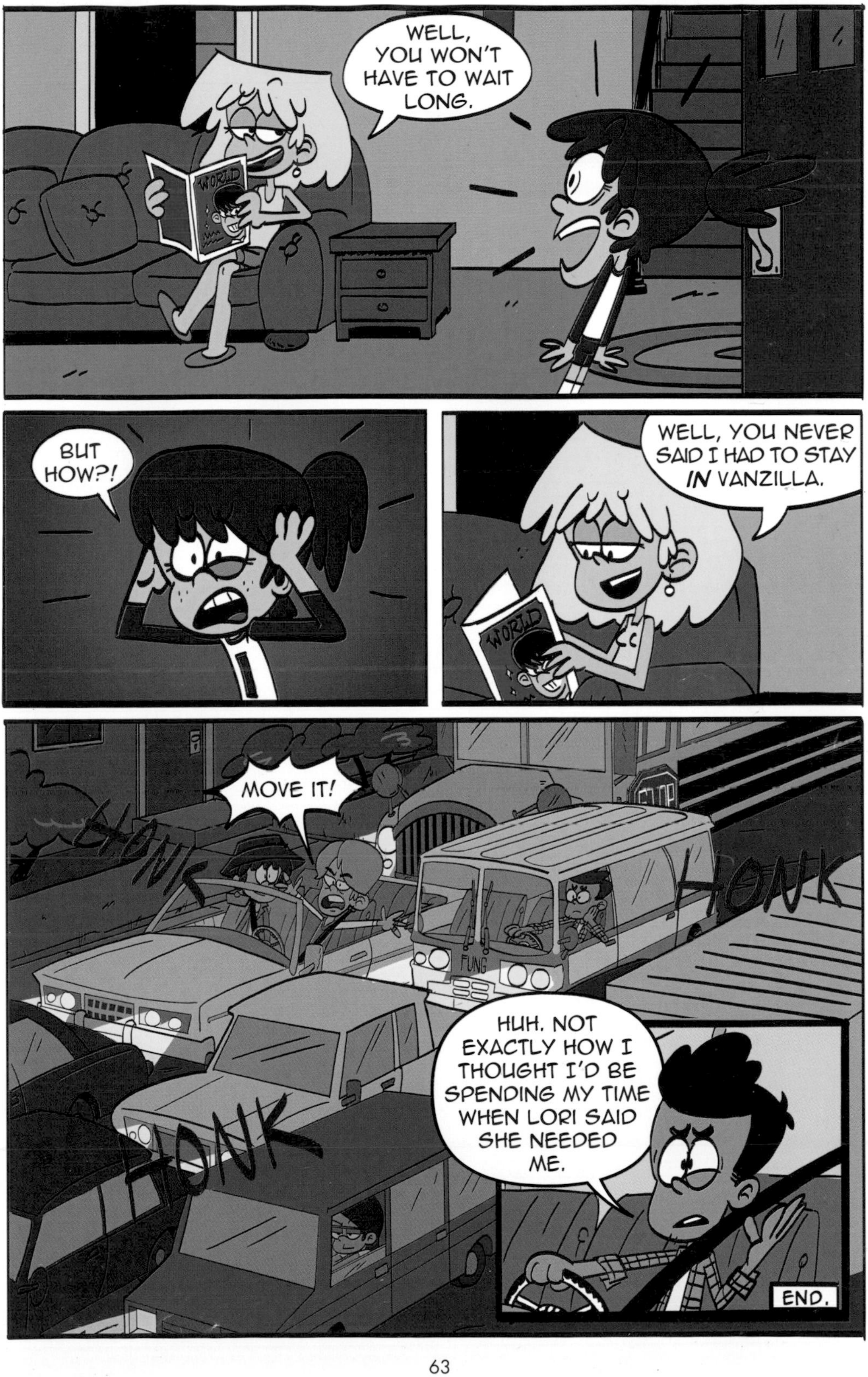
WELL, YOU WON'T HAVE TO WAIT LONG.
WORLD
BUT HOW?!
WELL, YOU NEVER SAID I HAD TO STAY *IN* VANZILLA.
MOVE IT!
HONK
HONK
FUNG
HONK
HUH. NOT EXACTLY HOW I THOUGHT I'D BE SPENDING MY TIME WHEN LORI SAID SHE NEEDED ME.
END.

WATCH OUT FOR PAPERCUTZ

Welcome to the sibling-spotlighting, sixth, sensational THE LOUD HOUSE graphic novel, "Loud and Proud," which immediately follows the events of THE LOUD HOUSE #5 "After Dark," which featured their all-night-long antics. As usual, it's from Papercutz—those shoved—and stepped-upon subway commuters dedicated to publishing graphic novels for all ages. I'm Jim Salicrup, the Editor-in-Chief and former carpool lane passenger here to thank some of the behind-the-scenes folks responsible for creating THE LOUD HOUSE comics…

First there are the writers who have taken time out of scripting shows for The Loud House TV show, to craft comicbook scripts for us: Sammie Crowley, Kevin Sullivan, Whitney Wetta. Not to mention Andrew Brooks, Angela Entzminger, and Hannah Watanabe-Rocco from *The Loud House* production team all returning to pen new stories for *THE LOUD HOUSE.*

Then we have a couple of new contributors, cartoonist Suzannah Rowntree, one of our former Papercutz Associate Editors, and Melissa Klenowski, ex-Papercutz Editorial Intern making her professional comics drawing debut. Animation alumni Angela Zhang, Scott Tuft, and Brian Smith also each join the ranks while *THE LOUD HOUSE* artists Agny Innocente, Ida Hem, Colton Davis, Erin Hyde, Gizelle Orbino, and Isaiah Kim all make their triumphant returns! Jordan Koch makes a guest appearance contributing the all-new cover!

In *THE LOUD HOUSE* #5, the super-talented Ida Hem lettered every story, but between her daytime duties at Rise of the *Teenage Mutant Ninja Turtles* and drawing "The Good Old Days," she wasn't able to letter this volume as well. Fortunately, Wilson Ramos Jr., who letters such Papercutz graphic novels as GERONIMO STILTON REPORTER, HOTEL TRANSYLVANIA, and many others, was able to step in and letter almost every story.

And all of the above worked with Papercutz editor (and champion of supporting characters everywhere) Jeff Whitman, under the watchful eyes of Joan Hilty, the Nickelodeon Comics Editor (and a very talented cartoonist herself), Dana Cluverius and Mollie Freilich at *The Loud House* show, and of course, yours truly. Together we can all be as crazed and frantic as the Loud family, but we're united in our love of *THE LOUD HOUSE* and the process of creating fun comics with these irresistible characters.

But most of all we want to thank you! Your support is what makes everything possible. So, if you're enjoying The Loud House TV series and comics, we sincerely thank you, and hope you come back for *THE LOUD HOUSE* #7 "The Struggle is Real"!

Thanks Jim

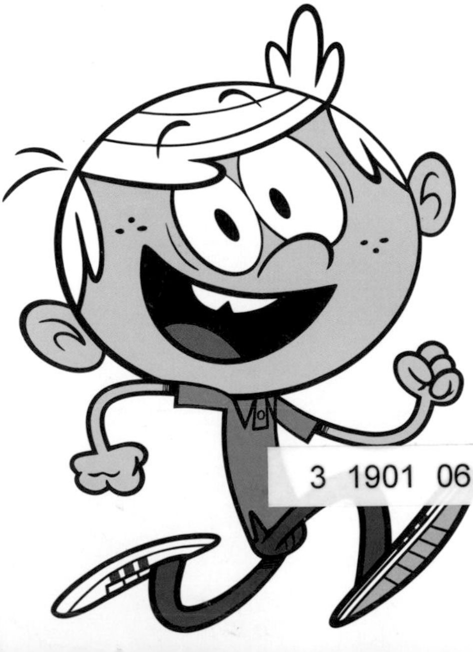

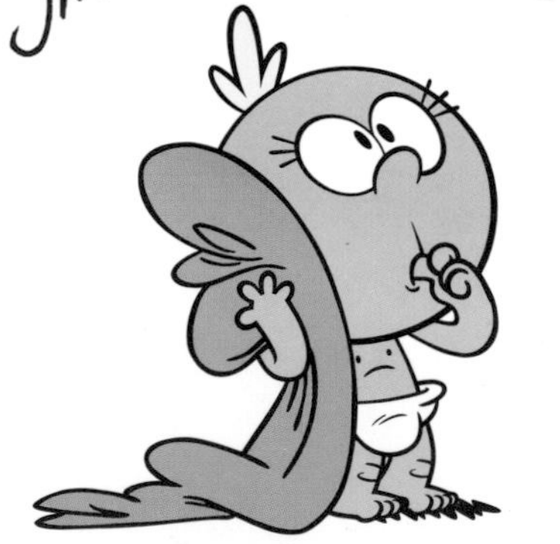

STAY IN TOUCH!

EMAIL:	salicrup@papercutz.com
WEB:	papercutz.com
	@papercutzgn
INSTAGRAM:	@papercutzgn
FACEBOOK:	PAPERCUTZGRAPHICNOVELS
FANMAIL:	Papercutz, 160 Broadway, Suite 700, East Wing, New York, NY 10038